The Body

The Renaissance Society at The University of Chicago

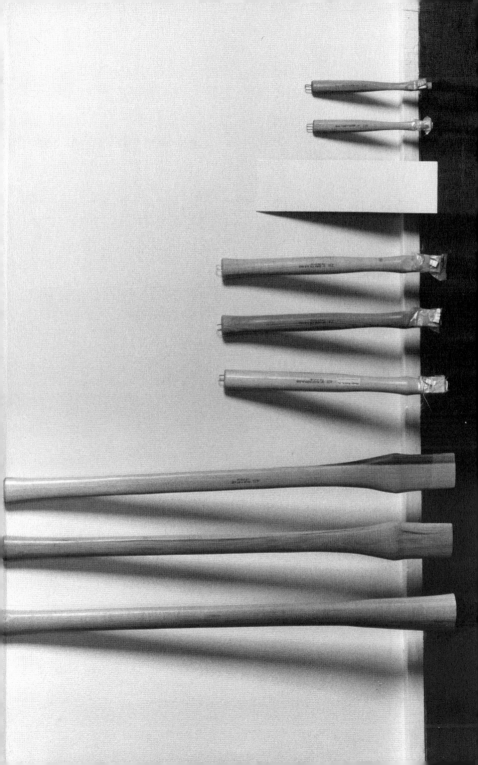

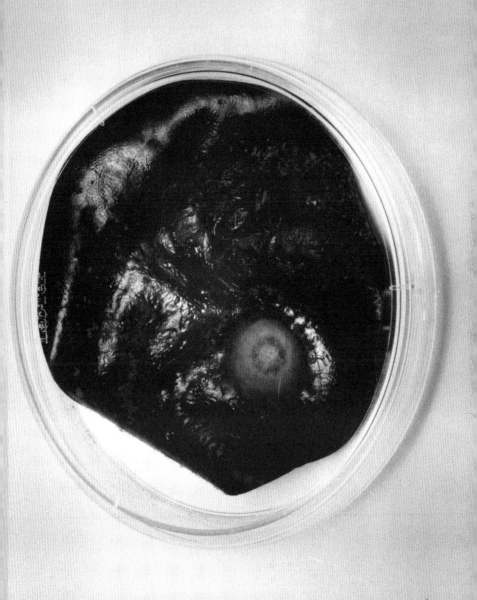

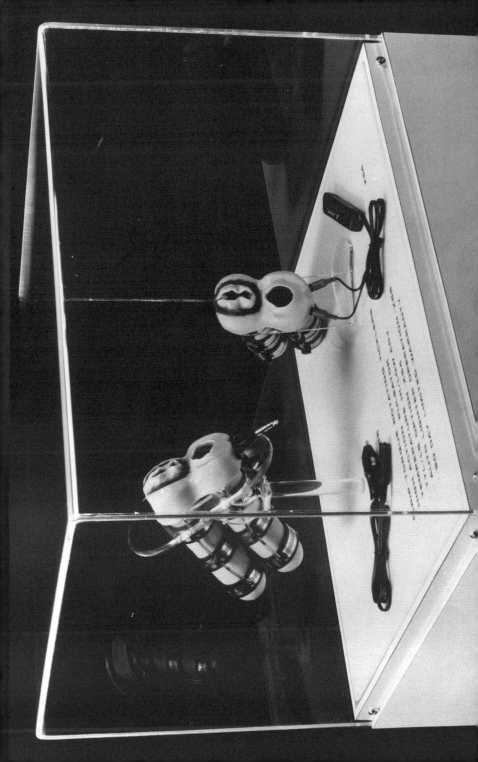

te ⌣ *ta*

1

For reasons I don't want to go into, I decided to commit suicide.

The poet Marshak has these marvelous lines: *'Death came like a court order and seized possession of life.'* Death came to me, too, like a court order. I chose not to resist the summons.

Having no experience with suicide, I turned to fiction. Emma Bovary poisoned herself. As far as I remember from Flaubert, it was a long and painful process, and — in view of the state of medical science at the time — uncertain. You could be saved and then a letter might be written to the courts: the life of every member of society belongs to society, and you have no right to do violence to public property. So poisoning was unsuitable.

Shooting yourself was not realistic. Pistols had gone out of everyday use. This wasn't the nineteenth century, when every self-respecting person had a gun in the way that nowadays they had a cigarette lighter or a ball-point pen.

What was the alternative? Hanging yourself was unaesthetic. Jumping out of a window was too frightening. I wanted death to enter unobtrusively, to take me gently by the hand and lead me away, as though to happiness, as though into the arms of a loved one after a long separation. After all, that's what it was. Life was separation from eternity. I came from eternity and would return to it. Life was a pause between two eternities and it was up to me, and no one else, how long that pause was to last.

I asked myself: 'What do I love most of all?'

Most of all I liked to be glad. But no one had ever died of gladness. I also loved sleeping. Perhaps I should die in my sleep?

You could take sleeping pills, but sleeping pills were sold only one dose at a time, and you would have to collect doses for a whole week before you had enough. In a week you might change your mind or be distracted.

There was another way: to fall permanently asleep. That is, to freeze to death. Like the coachman in the song, who was snow-bound in the far-off steppes. Survivors say that at first you feel cold, then warm, then you have blissful dreams.

Please don't think I'm joking or playing some kind of game. I was not feeling at all cheerful — although, to be honest, I was not sad either. I didn't feel sorry for myself. I was in a practical mood. I recalled two lines from Bella Akhmadulina:

Let us endure the death of both of us,
Without a show of pity and without a fuss.

My head was stuffed with lines from modern poetry. I knew whole poems by heart; for example: "I do not want to know where I can be alone." But enough about poetry. I had more serious matters to deal with.

I went into the bathroom, started the shower and stepped in. I stood there long enough to get completely wet, then wrapped myself in a big, fluffy bath-towel and went out on to the balcony. Into thirty degrees below freezing.

I felt as if I had stepped into a bonfire, like Joan of Arc. Extreme cold, apparently, burns you. Very high and very low temperatures produce the same effect. It was unbearable standing there; it was like a fire, but without the smoke. I suspect that the blissful dreams are a lie, but to know for certain you had to wait to see if the blissful dreams came true. To wait you had to be patient. And patience required the right mood. Whatever you were doing, the main thing was always to be in the right mood.

My hair instantly turned into a cluster of glass pipettes, my eyelashes became long, white and fluffy. Up in the black sky, the moon hung like an uncooked pancake. I was leaving, but the moon would stay. People would continue to look up from the earth at the moon, and the pancake would go on lying to them that it was meaningful. The city glittered with lighted windows. Behind each window there was an idiot — or several idiots together.

A sound of clumsy rustling came from one side, as though a bear was trying to climb in. Perhaps this was the start of a blissful dream. But it was nothing of the sort. A hulking man was climbing from the balcony next door over on to mine. A burglar most likely. He'd been robbing the neighboring flat, but the owners had come back unexpectedly, and now he had to get away. Or perhaps he was a heroic but luckless lover. He had come to see another man's wife and, suddenly surprised by the husband, had decided to risk his life on the balcony rather that risk it in a show-down.

Perhaps he was a murderous maniac. There were such types. For me, personally, the appearance of a murderous maniac was a stroke of luck, because he would greatly speed up my intended move from here to *there*; it would be like taking a taxi. You must agree, though: it's one thing to depart this life by your own efforts and quite another to be shoved out of it against your will, even in a taxi.

I screamed with all my might, although I hadn't much might left.

The robber saw me. I was barefoot, encrusted with ice and wrapped in a towel. He stood there like a lamp-post, with the same degree of cast-iron immobility.

'What are you doing here?' he asked, astonished, in an educated voice.

'And what are *you* doing here?' I asked.

My lips couldn't move, and I spoke the words like a ventriloquist.

'I want to go through your flat onto the staircase. May I?'

'You may,' I said graciously.

'And you?'

'What about me?'

'Won't you see me out? I don't know how your locks work.'

Obviously not a burglar. Otherwise the locks wouldn't have bothered him.

'All right,' I agreed and stepped off the balcony into my room.

The light was on. I hadn't turned it off before dying. My towel had frozen and was like a sheet of tin.

The robber followed me and was clearly baffled.

'What were you doing out there?' he inquired, overcome by curiosity.

'It was too hot in here.'

'Do you practice yoga?'

'Yes,' I agreed; it saved explanations.

'Aren't you cold?'

'No. I'm used to it.'

We went to the door. With rigid fingers I opened the lock and, before letting the robber out, I turned and looked at him. Again I felt a burning sensation, as I had from the cold. I recognized him.

'Are you Onisimov?'

'No, I'm not Onisimov. Who's he?'

'Oh...just somebody.'

Onisimov was my first love. I was fourteen. Our school was across the street from a student hostel, and the windows of our classroom overlooked a room occupied by two jolly students. During break-time the girls would hang over the window-sill and shout stupid, cheerful things at the boys below. One was Onisimov; he actually shouted out: 'I'm Onisimov!' He had blond hair, nice regular features, long arms and strong hands. I've always remembered him.

Love for Onisimov went into my heart like a needle of happiness, but I didn't show my love in any way. I never hung over the window-sill and shouted. I stood behind the others and stared, unable to tear myself away. No doubt he never saw me. Or had an inkling of my love.

In class I would sit with my neck twisted, looking out at Onisimov's window. Sometimes he would appear briefly, and then my heart turned a somersault, gently detaching itself as though in a state of weightlessness, and floated down to my stomach. I almost fainted.

When I moved up the next year, our windows looked out on the other side of the building. It all ended. We never got to know each other, he never had a chance to disappoint me and my love for him remained imperishable. Like the honey in the sarcophagus. Recently they dug up a pharaoh from the depths of several millennia. Not even the pharaoh's buttons had survived, but an amphora of honey was still intact. You could have sat down and had it for tea. Such was my love for Onisimov.

I can't say I've waited for him all my life. He couldn't have come to me, because he didn't know me. In those days the queen of the window-sill was Rita Nosikova, a red-haired beauty, while I stood at the back wearing spectacles, with my stockings twisted, my head stuffed with poetry. He didn't see me, and naturally never guessed at my love. But I remember him; he was part of my life. And the fact that he had appeared at precisely this fateful moment was on the one hand improbable, but on the other — entirely natural.

'No. I am not Onisimov,' he repeated. 'People are always mixing me up with somebody else. I always seem to look like another person.'

He really was like Onisimov, but I could have been mistaken. A lot of water had flowed under the bridge since I was fourteen. And I had seen Onisimov only from a distance, across the street.

I looked at the man's hands. Hands like his could never steal or kill, but they might caress.

'Well, goodbye,' said Not-Onisimov. 'Please excuse me.'

I shut the door after him. I didn't want to return to the balcony. The mood had gone.

I went into the bathroom, ran a bathful of hot water, got into it and began slowly to thaw out, like a chicken taken out of the freezer. The warmth went into me gradually, in layers, penetrating deeper as I bathed. I felt the warmth as if it were happiness — so real, I could have touched it with my hand.

Having thawed out, I reached for some Green Apple shampoo, washed my hair and dried it with a hand drier. The stream of hot air blew around my face. I scraped off some old nail varnish with my finger-nail and gave myself a fresh manicure. I put on my wedding dress: white embroidery on white muslin. It was made out of Yugoslav curtain-material and had been incredibly expensive when I bought it, though today the price would be reasonable. I had worn it once in my life, for my wedding. Since then it had been hanging in my wardrobe like an exhibit in a museum of ethnography, a reflection of my history and my glorious past.

Having dressed myself like a bride, I took an opened bottle of champagne out of the refrigerator, sat down at the kitchen table and turned on the gas taps — all four burners and the oven. There was a strong smell of garlic. My head seemed to fill with gas and felt light.

Don't think I'm mad. I was simply like an airplane that had run out of fuel and had started to glide. Its center of gravity was displaced and it went into a dive. That was my state at the time. I was outside myself.

I poured out some champagne and drank. The walls of the kitchen shuddered and started going round in a slow waltz rhythm, with heavy stress on one beat. I wanted to get up and circle in time with the walls. I heard a ring at the door. I decided the ringing was in my ears, but ringing in your ears never sounds so insistent and panicky. The ringing stopped and I heard knocking: fists were hammering on the door, feet kicking it; then someone stepped back, took a run and hit it with his whole body. I realized that if I didn't get up at once and open it, my door would come crashing down.

I went into the hall, slid back the bolts and took off the chain. On the threshold stood Not-Onisimov. He saw me in the white dress and went as rigid as a lamp-post for the second time. Then he firmly pushed me aside and marched into the kitchen, as though he were not a caller but in his own home. Not-Onisimov turned off all the gas taps and flung open the window. Frosty air strode into the kitchen; it was too heavy to float in.

'Why did you turn on the gas?' Not-Onisimov asked sternly.

'I was trying to get warm,' I replied.

'One moment you're too hot, the next you're too cold,' he said, displeased.

'What business is it of yours? Why are you shuttling in and out of here? First you come in by the window, then by the door.'

'Because I don't like the look of you.' He stared me straight in the eye, and I took off my glasses so that I wouldn't see him clearly. 'Why are you behaving like this? Has somebody upset you?'

'I don't ask *you* questions like this.'

'You can if you like.'

'Why were you escaping over the balcony? Did her husband come?'

'Yes.' Not-Onisimov confirmed my suspicion, nodding his head. 'How did you know?'

'From all those jokes. Typical situation. He arrived — and at the wrong time.'

'Yes. We hadn't made any arrangement.'

'Obviously. You don't have to explain.'

'I didn't want to see him. The fact is, I've killed his wife.'

This was an unexpected twist to the typical situation. I put on my glasses, and having refocused I looked at my uninvited visitor. 'Out of jealously?' I inquired.

'I'm a doctor. Surgeon. I operated on her.'

'Ah, I see ... A botched job.'

'Botched job? It was the operation of the century! Only De Baeky has done one like it! Have you heard of De Baeky?'

'No,' I confessed.

Not-Onisimov looked at me with contempt, as though De Baeky were Shakespeare. Incidentally, I haven't read Shakespeare. I see his plays in the theatre.

'De Baeky is the foremost surgeon in the world. He proposed implanting a Teflon valve into the heart. All valves before him were ball-and-socket. The ball functioned well enough, but it made such a noise that the patient sounded like a clock. You could hear it ticking from five meters away. Then there were the so-called petal valves. Later they tried implanting the valve from a pig's heart. De Baeky was the first to suggest Teflon. Do you know what Teflon is?'

'No.'

'You don't know anything. It's a super-durable synthetic material. It's used in non-stick frying pans, it lets you fry without fat. A Teflon valve will never wear out.'

'Like one's first love,' I thought. If De Baeky had operated on that pharaoh they would have found a valve as well as the honey.

'Did you sew a valve like that into her?' I asked, guessing.

'I didn't sew it in. I glued it in. I went further than De Baeky. For five years I've been working with a group of scientists to develop an organic glue that is gradually absorbed by the body's tissues. The valve settles in without a single stitch and without any traumatic effect on the heart muscles. But the chief advantage is time. A valve implant used to take five hours. Now it takes forty minutes. Like taking out an appendix. I have advanced surgery by a hundred years. I have practically relieved people of the fear of heart disease. We'll be able to mend hearts the way we mend cars in a repair workshop. I phoned De Baeky. He's invited me to see him, along with my patient. But the trouble is, she's not recovering.'

'Why not?'

'She's not fighting. She says she's tired. When a person doesn't want to live, it's fatal. Because it's all up here.' Not-Onisimov tapped his forehead. 'I once had a case in which I operated on a very severe ulcer. I was convinced it wouldn't be successful. The patient was a lorry-driver, who drove a refrigerated truck full of fish. He used to swallow fish whole, like a cat. And he drank, in my opinion... But that's not the point. I was afraid he'd die on the operating table. But he didn't. I completed the operation. An hour later I went to see him in the resuscitation unit, and his bed was empty. I looked under the bed; I thought he might have fallen out. He wasn't there. The attendants ran around looking for him. I went into the toilet—and there he was, sitting and smoking. His brain hadn't taken in the seriousness of the operation. Believe it or not, he recovered. But this woman's case... In America an operation like hers would cost one and a half million dollars.'

Not-Onisimov poured himself some champagne and drank it. 'Want some?' he asked me, although it was I and not he who should have offered it.

'Thanks.' I sat down at the table.

Not-Onisimov sat down too; he didn't drink any more, but leaned his head on his hand, looking mournful. I noticed the bald patch on the crown of his head and a needle of pity went into my heart.

'It's not your fault,' I said with conviction. 'You've done everything you could. But if she...It's up to her now.'

'There's no such thing as an operation in the abstract, detached from the patient. It's much better for a patient to survive after a bad operation than for him or her to die after a good operation ... And her husband came to say thank you. Brought me a bottle of brandy. French.'

'So that's *your* flat next door?' I was amazed.

'Of course. I live on the staircase next to yours.'

'I've never seen you.'

'I've never seen you, either.'

'So the husband is still there, sitting in your flat.'

'I don't know. Probably.'

'But why couldn't you have gone out by the door?'

'Well, it's awkward to walk out when someone comes to see you. So I just disappeared. Without any explanations.'

'Yes, but even so, it's an awkward situation. You'll have to go back.'

'I've got to be at the hospital.'

I didn't understand. 'What's the time?'

'Doesn't matter. I must be near her. Or rather, I can't let myself be anywhere else.'

'Well, go then...'

'I can't leave you.'

'Why not?'

'I've told you: I don't like the look of you.'

'But you can't be in two places at once.'

'Will you come with me?' asked Not-Onisimov.

I put on a leather coat over my wedding dress, took off my gilded slippers and stuck my feet into a pair of felt boots. Not-Onisimov was wearing only a sweater and jeans.

'Can't I give you something to wear for the cold?' I asked.

'What have you got?'

'Nothing. I haven't got any men's clothes.'

'In that case I'll take a blanket,' said Not-Onisimov, inventively. 'Do you have any blankets?'

I had two bed-covers, an eiderdown and a quilt. I gave him the eiderdown. Not-Onisimov wrapped himself to the top of his head. He looked very good in the eiderdown.

The hospital consisted of a group of white buildings, like doctors' white coats, and we entered one and climbed the stairs to the second floor.

'Why do you have to replace people's heart-valves?' I asked.

'The old one breaks down. When I saw her valve, I couldn't understand why she was still alive.'

'Why do they break down?'

'Not "they"; it. The mitral valve. Between the auricle and the ventricle.'

'But why do they break down? From stress?'

'From rheumatoid assault.'

'Assault? What's that?'

'You're not a doctor. You wouldn't understand.'

We walked into an office. Not-Onisimov threw my eiderdown onto a couch and took a white coat out of the cupboard and left the room, only to return immediately. 'Come with me!' he commanded. He was obviously afraid of leaving me alone.

A dim light was burning in the corridor. It was deserted. The patients were asleep. '*Silent, still as water in a bowl, life lay sleeping.*' I've left out 'her'. It should be: 'Her *life lay sleeping.*'

She was not asleep. She was in a single-bed room, staring at the ceiling. It was impossible to determine her age: somewhere between twenty and fifty. She did not react when we came in.

'Alla!' Not-Onisimov called out her name.

She continued staring upwards.

Not-Onisimov lifted her limp arm from her chest and took her pulse, then put her arm back.

'Alla!' Not-Onisimov said quietly. 'Please.'

Alla didn't hear. Or didn't want to hear. She conveyed the cold indifference of outer space.

Not-Onisimov tried to say something but couldn't. He turned around and went out of the room like a blind man. I had the feeling that he would burst into tears. He had forgotten me in his despair.

A needle of pity went right through me.

'Please...' I repeated softly.

I sat down on the bed in such a way as to interrupt her gaze, to catch her eye. She saw me in my white wedding dress and felt boots and evidently concluded that it was Death who had appeared in this strange garb, but not even Death aroused her interest.

'I understand you,' I whispered fervently. 'I understand ... You've been in so much pain, I don't know how you kept on living. You're tired and you want to rest at any cost. Even at the cost of falling asleep for ever. You want a rest from pain, from people, from everything that life is, because your life is nothing but heart aches. No one can suffer so long. You've had too much. Your spring has broken. I understand. But you're not alone, Alla. Your doctor, who has mended you, is on your side. Hundreds, thousands of patients who need your recovery as a guarantee — they're all praying for you. And Dr. De Baeky is on your side too, and the whole of America; they're cheering for you. People get sick there too, you know. In America an operation like yours costs a million and a half dollars. Only a millionaire can afford it, and not even every millionaire. Yours was done free. And still you're ... being obstinate. Maybe you don't care for the rest of the human race any longer — you may not care about America or De Baeky. But the people who love you are backing you up. Right now your husband can't sleep; he's going out of his mind. You simply haven't the right. Can you hear me?'

'Who are you?' Alla asked softly.

'No one,' I said.

'I'm not dreaming about you, am I?'

'No. I exist. I'm real.'

I bent low over Alla and my glasses fell off onto her face. She raised her hand, picked up my glasses and put them on.

'You really are there,' she breathed. 'I can see you now.' She could see and hear me, and her attention sent a cold shiver through me. I had completely forgotten about my troubles and about my reasons (which I don't want to tell you about) for standing on the balcony.

'You mustn't think of only yourself. You mustn't love only yourself or pity yourself. Otherwise your center of gravity will be upset.'

'What will be upset?' asked Alla.

'Everything. The whole solar system. You don't have the right.'

'What do you want me to do?' Alla asked weakly.

'I only want you to go to the lavatory.'

'What for?'

'To have a smoke.'

'I don't want to. I can't.'

'But you don't know whether you can or not. People don't know their own potential.'

I put my arms round Alla's shoulders and started to lift her up. She clasped my neck and let me guide her.

'My valve won't come loose, will it?' Alla asked. She was afraid for her life, and that was a good sign.

'No, it won't,' I assured her. 'But it'll get a bit of a surprise.'

She was up. We walked slowly out of the room and into the corridor, I with my white wedding dress, Alla in her white patient's gown with the hospital stamp on the back. We clutched each other like a pair of white ghosts, and I had the feeling that if we were to jump in the air we would take off and float. Her weakness flowed into me, and my gladness flowed into her, the gladness that I love more than anything else on earth and would like to die of. But at that moment I didn't want to die. My earlier mood had gone, vanished. I wanted only one thing: to keep walking with Alla, my arms around her, to carry this stranger's fragile life, like a butterfly, in the palm of my hand.

The corridor was empty. A nurse was dozing on a sofa. An alarm clock was giving out a hypnotic tick and the sound, like a cricket's song, carried through the corridors.

Not-Onisimov emerged from the office where he had dressed. He saw us and did his lamp-post act again.

'Good evening,' Alla greeted him, although it was almost

morning.

'What are you doing here?' was all that Not-Onisimov could think of saying.

'We're going for a smoke,' I said.

Not-Onisimov dashed towards us, took Alla's arm and felt her pulse. Then he turned to me, with an astonished look on his face, and asked: 'How did you do it?'

The alarm clock rang. It was six o'clock in the morning. Time for the first injections.

The nurse got up from the sofa. She was a broad-hipped, broad-shouldered girl in round spectacles. She looked like a denizen of the forest, like the strange, fairy-tale creature Ukhti-Tukhti. I had heard the story as a child, but to this day I have never understood who or what Ukhti-Tukhti was. A chicken, perhaps, or a hedgehog.

'Here,' ordered Not-Onisimov.

The taxi-driver stopped the car outside Not-Onisimov's entrance.

'I must sleep,' Not-Onisimov explained as he paid off the cab. 'I haven't slept for five days. I'm going to bed now and I shall sleep like a corpse.'

We clambered out of the taxi. The driver looked at Not-Onisimov in his eiderdown with utter amazement. I wondered what he was thinking. I moved towards my entrance.

'Where are you going?' Not-Onisimov called out. 'Come up to my place.'

He called me as one calls a dog, and I went up to him like a dog, with the same degree of trust and ingenuity.

'But you're going to bed,' I reminded him.

'Well, so what? You can go to bed too. We've even got your eiderdown with us. So you can go to sleep under it.' Not-Onisimov took me by the hand and led the way.

'I can't sleep without a night-dress,' I objected, weakly.

'Can't help you there. Haven't got any women's things. Go to bed in the dress you're wearing.'

We went into the elevator. Not-Onisimov leaned back against

the rail, shut his eyes and fell asleep standing up, like a horse. I pressed the necessary button. I knew the floor, because we were neighbors and lived on the same level.

I guided Not-Onisimov to his front door. Not being fully awake, he tried to open it but the key wouldn't turn in the lock.

'What the hell?' said Not-Onisimov, puzzled.

I heard a rustling from inside. The door swung open. A tousled, red-shirted man of indeterminate age stood on the threshold. I guessed he was Alla's husband. He might have been thirty or he might have been fifty. Either he was thirty and was looking bad, which was natural in his situation, or he was pushing fifty and looking very good.

'Are you still here?' said Not-Onisimov, not sounding surprised.

'Where else should I be?' The husband sounded surprised.

They were silent for a moment and looked at each other.

'Come in,' said the husband. 'Take off your things.'

We went in. I took off my coat, Not-Onisimov threw off the eiderdown and rubbed his wooden-stiff fingers. His expression was one of exhaustion and happiness. He looked satisfied, like the legendary hero Alyosha Popovich after doing battle with the Tartars.

'Let's have that brandy of yours,' said Not-Onisimov grandly. 'We can drink it now. We have the right. We've earned it.'

'But I'm afraid I've already drunk it,' said the husband, embarrassed. 'You were away for so long.'

'All of it?' Not-Onisimov was dismayed.

'Well, yes,' the husband confirmed guiltily. 'I waited and waited.'

'In that case you can go home,' said Not-Onisimov, dismissing him. He rubbed his hands like a man of action. Not-Onisimov had operated successfully. Not-Onisimov's life was a success. No more and no less. 'Go home,' he said.

'Me?' the husband countered, prodding his red-checked chest with his index finger.

'Both of you.' He turned to me. 'You too. Go and get undressed in your normal way and you will sleep normally. It's uncomfortable sleeping in your clothes, anyway.'

'Why are you kicking me out?'

'Because I don't like the look of you.'

He came up to me. Took off my glasses. Began to survey my short-sighted features as though stroking me with his eyes. My heart turned a somersault, gently detaching itself from its moorings, and floated in a state of weightlessness.

'I think I've seen you somewhere before.'

'Of course you have; we're neighbors, after all.'

'No. Before that.'

Perhaps when I had been standing behind the other girls. Behind Rita Nosikova's broad, laughing face.

'I don't want to go all the way downstairs and all the way up again. Can I go out over your balcony?'

'You can,' allowed Not-Onisimov. 'But I'll help you.'

We went onto the balcony. He offered me his strong, handsome, talented hand. I leaned against it and confidently climbed up the balcony rail. The city was asleep and dreaming its predawn dreams.

How many times in my life have I stretched out my hand in help, and to how many people, I wonder? And when I have needed help, none of them have ever been around. The one who did happen to be around was a total stranger, who by chance dropped — literally — at my feet. Therefore the principle of 'You scratch my back, I'll scratch yours' doesn't work, because goodness is unselfish. You help me, I'll help someone else, he'll help another person — and so on through time and space. Let the chain not be broken.

Alla's husband came out onto the balcony too and solicitously draped my eiderdown around Not-Onisimov. The husband was taking care of Not-Onisimov. Not-Onisimov was supporting me. I had supported Alla. Alla was all mankind, and mankind, God willing, would stretch out a hand to her husband. And then the whole world would be joined up in a single Grand Chain.

The sky was lighting up, the black turning to grey, and the moon, having lost the chic dark background which showed it off so well, had faded and was neutral, uninteresting — neither good nor bad. The houses looked like a photographic negative: the walls were light, the windows dark. And it seemed to me that behind each window there slept a genius, or even several geniuses together.

———————————

2

A young man asked a father for his daughter's hand, and received it in a box — her left hand.

Father: 'You asked for her hand and you have it. But it is my opinion that you wanted other things and took them.'

Young man: 'Whatever do you mean?'

Father: 'Whatever do you think I mean? You cannot deny that I am more honorable than you, because you took something from my family without asking, whereas when you asked for my daughter's hand, I gave it.'

Actually, the young man had not done anything dishonorable. The father was merely suspicious and had a dirty mind. The father could legally make the young man responsible for his daughter's upkeep and soak him financially. The young man could not deny that he had the daughter's hand — even though in desperation he had now buried it, after kissing it. But it was becoming two weeks old.

The young man wanted to see the daughter, and made an effort, but was quite blocked by besieging tradesmen. The daughter was signing cheques with her right hand. Far from bleeding to death, she was going ahead at full speed.

The young man announced in newspapers that she had quit his bed and board. But he had to prove that she had ever enjoyed them. It was not yet 'a marriage' on paper, or in the church. Yet there was no doubt that he had her hand, and had signed a receipt for it when the package had been delivered.

'Her hand in *what*?' the young man demanded of the police, in despair and down to his last penny. 'Her hand is buried in my garden.'

'You are a criminal to boot? Not merely disorganized in your way of life, but a psychopath? Did you by chance cut off your wife's hand?'

'I did not, and she is not even my wife!'

'He has her hand, and yet she is not his wife!' scoffed the men of the law. 'What shall we do with him? He is unreasonable, maybe even insane.'

'Lock him up in an asylum. He is also broke, so it will have to be a State Institution.'

So the young man was locked up, and once a month the girl whose hand he had received came to look at him through the wire barrier, like a dutiful wife. And like most wives, she had nothing to say. But she smiled prettily. His job provided a small pension now, which she was getting. Her stump was concealed in a muff.

Because the young man became too disgusted with her to look at her, he was placed in a more disagreeable ward, deprived of books and company, and he went really insane.

When he became insane, all that had happened to him, the asking for and receiving his beloved's hand, became intelligible to him. He realized what a horrible mistake, crime even, he had been guilty of in demanding such a barbaric thing as a girl's hand.

He spoke to his captors, saying that now he understood his mistake.

'What mistake? To ask for a girl's hand? So did I, when I married.'

The young man, feeling now he was insane beyond repair, since he could make contact with nothing, refused to eat for many days, and at last lay on his bed with his face to the wall, and died.

3

It happened simply, without pretense. For reasons that need not be explained, the town was suffering from a meat shortage. Everyone was alarmed, and rather bitter comments were heard; revenge was even spoken of. But, as always, the protests did not develop beyond threats, and soon the afflicted townspeople were devouring the most diverse vegetables.

Only Mr. Ansaldo didn't follow the order of the day. With great tranquility, he began to sharpen an enormous kitchen knife and then, dropping his pants to his knees, he cut a beautiful fillet from his left buttock. Having cleaned and dressed the fillet with salt and vinegar, he passed it through the broiler and finally fried it in the big pan he used on Sundays for making tortillas. He sat at the table and began to savor his beautiful fillet. Just then, there was a knock at the door: it was Ansaldo's neighbor coming to vent his frustrations. . . . Ansaldo, with an elegant gesture, showed his neighbor the beautiful fillet. When his neighbor asked about it, Ansaldo simply displayed his left buttock. The facts were laid bare. The neighbor, overwhelmed and moved, left without saying a word to return shortly with the mayor of the town. The latter expressed to Ansaldo his intense desire that his beloved towns-people be nourished—as was Ansaldo—by drawing on their private reserves, that is to say, each from their own meat. The issue was soon resolved, and after outbursts from the well edu-cated, Ansaldo went to the main square of the town to offer—as he characteristically phrased it—"a practical demonstration for the masses."

Once there, he explained that each person could cut two fillets, from their left buttock, just like the flesh-colored plaster model he had hanging from a shining meathook. He showed how to cut two fillets not one, for if he had cut one beautiful fillet from his own left buttock, it was only right that no one should consume one fillet fewer. Once these points were cleared up, each person began to slice two fillets from his left buttock. It was a glorious spectacle, but it is requested that descriptions not be given out. Calculations were made concerning how long the town would enjoy the benefits of this meat. One distinguished physician predicted that a person weighing one hundred pounds (discounting viscera and the rest of the inedible organs) could eat meat for one hundred and forty days at the rate of half a pound a day. This calculation was, of course, deceptive. And what mattered was that each person could eat his beautiful fillet. Soon women were heard speaking of the advantages of Mr. Ansaldo's idea. For example, those who had devoured their breasts didn't need to cover their torsos with cloth, and their dresses reached just above the navel. Some women — though not all of them — no longer spoke at all, for they had gobbled up their tongues (which, by the way, is the delicacy of monarchs). In the streets, the most amusing scenes occurred: two women who had not seen each other for a long time were unable to kiss each other: they had both used their lips to cook up some very successful fritters. The prison warden could not sign a convict's death sentence because he had eaten the fleshy tips of his fingers, which, according to the best "gourmets" (of which the warden was one), gave rise to the well-worn phrase "finger-licking good."

There was some minor resistance. The ladies garment workers union registered their most formal protest with the appropriate authority, who responded by saying that it wasn't possible to create a slogan that might encourage women to patronize their tailors again. But the resistance was never significant, and did not in any way interrupt the townspeople's consumption of their own meat.

One of the most colorful events of that pleasant episode was the dissection of the town ballet dancer's last morsel of flesh.

Out of respect for his art, he had left his beautiful toes for last. His neighbors observed that he had been extremely restless for days. There now remained only the fleshy tip of one big toe. At that point he invited his friends to attend the operation. In the middle of a bloody silence, he cut off the last portion, and, without even warming it up, dropped it into the hole that had once been his beautiful mouth. Everyone present suddenly became very serious.

But life went on, and that was the important thing. And if, by chance...? Was it because of this that the dancer's shoes could now be found in one of the rooms of the Museum of Illustrious Memorabilia? It's only certain that one of the most obese men in town (weighing over four hundred pounds) used up his whole reserve of disposable meat in the brief space of fifteen days (he was extremely fond of snacks and sweetmeats, and besides, his metabolism required large quantities). After a while, no one could ever find him. Evidently, he was hiding.... But he was not the only one to hide; in fact, many others began to adopt identical behavior. And so, one morning Mrs. Orfila got no answer when she asked her son (who was in the process of devouring his left earlobe) where he had put something. Neither pleas nor threats did any good. The expert in missing persons was called in, but he couldn't produce anything more than a small pile of excrement on the spot where Mrs. Orfila swore her beloved son had just been sitting at the moment she was questioning him. But these little disturbances did not undermine the happiness of the inhabitants in the least. For how could a town that was assured of its subsistence complain? Hadn't the crisis of public order caused by the meat shortage been definitely resolved? That the population was increasingly dropping out of sight was but a postscript to the fundamental issue and did not affect the people's determination to obtain their vital sustenance. Was that postscript the price that the flesh exacted from each? But it would be petty to ask any more such inopportune questions, now that this thoughtful community was perfectly well fed.

4.

Their friend made ready for the two couples. The lovers would at last be united in the flesh. He had prepared everything with exquisite taste, insisting only that in exchange for the immense joy he was providing them everything must be consummated in absolute darkness and in the strictest silence. So, when the lovers arrived, he informed them that the lighted room where they stood was the last they would contemplate during their unforgettable, carnal night. Formal courtesies were exchanged, and they made their way through a small gallery to the immense doors that led, said the friend, to the two nuptial bedrooms.

Already the walk through the gallery had been consummated in absolute darkness. The friend (who had no need of light) announced that they had reached the entrance to human paradise, and that at his signal, the doors would open to admit the eternal lovers, separated until now by the inevitable tricks of fate.

Suddenly, a wave of terror animated them: it seems a gust of wind abruptly lifted the women's gowns. Terrorized, they abandoned their lovers and pressed themselves madly against the breast of the friend, who was standing in the center of that strange assembly. Smiling slightly, and without retracting his order, the friend took them by the wrists and spun them around so that each came to rest in the arms of the wrong lover. The men were waiting like well-trained stallions, silent and tense. Order was soon reestablished and at a signal from the friend, the doors opened and the crossed lovers passed through.

There, in the carnal chamber, they lavished the most refined and unprecedented caresses on each other. In grateful and loving respect for the vow they had taken, they did not even begin to utter a single sound, but made love until they drained (as they say) "the cup of pleasure." All the while, the friend remained in a lighted room, torn with anguish. Soon the lovers would leave their rooms, and, seeing the horrible switch, their love would be extinguished by the disturbing knowledge that it had been consummated with objects absolutely indifferent to them.

The friend began to think of various means of repairing the breach: he immediately rejected the idea of carrying the women to a common room, then restoring them (now properly switched) to their respective lovers. That was a partial solution; for example, either of the women might suspect that something was amiss in the passage from a dark room to a lighted one. Suddenly, the friend smiled. He clapped his hands and two servants appeared instantly. He whispered a few words into their ears and they disappeared, returning shortly armed with small golden needles and enormous silver scissors. The friend examined the instruments and immediately directed the servants to the nuptial doors. They entered and, groping in the darkness, took hold of the women and quickly cut off their tongues and poked out their eyes, then did the same to the men. Relieved of their tongues and eyes, they were brought before the friend, who was waiting for them in his well-lighted room.

There he let them know that, desiring to prolong that memorable, carnal night, he had ordered two of his servants, armed with needles and scissors, to take out their eyes and cut off their tongues. Hearing this statement the lovers immediately recovered their expressions of ineffable happiness and through their gestures let the friend know the profound gratitude that possessed them.

For years they lived in uninterrupted joy. Finally, the hour of their death arrived and, perfect lovers that they were, they were stricken by the same fatal ailment and died at the same moment. Learning of this, their friend smiled slightly and decided to bury them, restoring to each lover his beloved and thereby to each

beloved her lover. This he did, but in their ignorance, the lovers
joyfully continued their unforgettable, carnal night.

5

Casey is dipping across the room, stuffing clothes into a suitcase. He is hurt and angry and he's making predictions like "No one will ever care for you the way I do," and "You'll rue the day you let me go."

Rue? Nobody says rue anymore. That's a Shakespeare thing, rue.

Casey turns back the vocabulary clock when he feels threatened. He gets up close to my face, shouting about folly and denial. Blue veins swell beneath the flesh of his temples. I've never seen him this way.

Casey is upset because my father has returned, he's back with the living and I need to be in love with him.

My father left this world 19 years ago when his car hit a guard rail on the Onandogwa Parkway.

Most other men would have died right then and there but my father crawled out of the car and into the woods.

He crawled quite a way.

It took two days to find him.

When he died my father was 38 years old. That's young! He was 38 and I was 14 and we had a precious, unresolved love between us.

I've read a few cheap books, books in which the fathers aggressively force their sons to commit acts, ugly acts, saying "Take it now!" and, in one particular case "Chew that turd, boy."

But we weren't that way. That wasn't us. A man who crawls lame and broken over three miles of deciduous forest does not exactly follow a path that others have set for him. He could have crawled to a gas station a quarter of a mile in the other direction, but he didn't.

He was different. I'm different. We were different!

It is the desire for respect and status that tries to make us all the same, tries to press men flat and bitter like coins. My father tried his best to fight it but he lost his strength lining boilers all day. He'd return home from work ruddy and exhausted. Then he'd sit at the kitchen table and slap himself across the forehead saying "I'm so stupid, stupid, stupid," waiting, I suppose, for my mother to say "No you're not, Lance. It's just that you never had the opportunities that those other fellows had." She, of course, never said it.

"I'm so stupid, stupid, stupid," and she'd say "I think we've already established that fact," or "A little louder, I don't think they heard you over in Vestal Park."

I would push aside my plate then and say "No you're not stupid. I think you're the smartest man in the world."

Then my mother would grind out her cigarette and roll her eyes and say "Talk about stupid." And my father would look at me and hold his head in his hands and say "My God, it's hereditary."

But he was only kidding. He was a kidder. He needed someone to believe in him, that's all he needed. Hectored by the world and my mother he would leave the table sharp and moody and retire to the living room before finishing his meal.

"Mr Somebody!" she'd call out after him "Mr Get Up And Go." Then she would leave the house or shut herself off in the bedroom and my father would take off his shirt and pants and relax on the sofa in front of the TV. The boring shows would put him to sleep and he'd stretch out in his underpants: Hanes, size 34. Machine wash hot, tumble dry. Off white because my mother never bothered to wash them correctly, half the time just throwing them in cold water with the colors so that, to tell the absolute truth, they weren't off-white so much as off off-white. But not because they were dirty because they weren't necessarily dirty.

Nothing here is dirty.

He'd fall asleep on his stomach, his hands tucked beneath him, his crack just barely poking out from the top of the elastic and forming a vague line below it. Or sometimes, say, when the briefs were too loose, his crack would bite the fabric, making the line bold and unmistakable.

Or he'd fall asleep on his back with his legs spread apart, his hands inside the pouch — grabbing hold of himself because, I think, he felt so threatened by the world.

He needed someone to watch over him. Who else did he have but me?

I would wait until my mother's light was out and then I'd join him in my own underpants, a pair I'd made special by cutting away the back and sides.

My father was a very sound sleeper.

I would kneel on the floor, push my hair back from my face, and get up close. So close! And I'd think, I'd always think "Smell The Freshness!" which is what the detergent commercials used to say.

"Smell the Freshness!"

So close that what I saw was almost too big to fathom, like a billboard announcing something so fabulous that it didn't really need to be advertised as it could so easily sell itself. I would watch over him closely and then patiently and then, later, closely and not so patiently.

But I always cleaned up my mess.

My mother, once she saw some stains on the cushion and she said to him "What kind of shows have you been watching?"

Curious, because this was back before VCR's.

"What is it you watch that gets you so excited?" she asked him. "Tell me and I'll watch too."

The last night of his life, I'll never forget it. September 21, 1971. My father was asleep in front of Johnny Carson. Skitch Henderson was filling in for Ed McMahon and the guests were Robert Stack, Dianna Riggs, and Totie Fields. My father was sleeping on his back and I was leaning over him thinking how, up close, the hairs on his upper thighs strongly resembled an aerial view of the fire-ravaged forests of Montana.

"Quick men, rush to the fire line!"

Johnny Carson introduced his next guest, a snappily dressed chimp who played the role of a private eye on a popular Saturday morning TV show. Totie Fields saw the chimp advancing from the wings and screamed out "WE LOVE YOU, LANCE!" And my father, hearing his own name associated with love, woke up. And he looked at me with my hard penis in my hand, and he looked at the TV set where Totie Fields was shaking and heaving and peppering a monkey's face with kisses, and he looked back at me and he said "I think we need to find you someone to talk to."

And the next day he died and two days later they found his body in the woods. Birds had pecked out his eyes. Can you believe that? Birds! Everyone thinks they're so adorable with their migratory patterns and clumsy nests but birds are base and cunning and capable of things that put the rest of us to shame.

When I first met Casey I thought of my father saying "I think we need to find you someone to talk to." Because, for a while, I could talk to Casey. But now that my father is back Casey has become hard and bitter, making threats and questioning my judgement.

But I know it's my father up there.

Casey says, and he's right, that I've been wrong before.

True. A few years ago I was convinced that Fleet Lockhart, bag boy at Food Carnival, was my father. My mistake. It's just that Fleet looked like my father might have looked when he was sixteen if he'd had acne and very yellow hair braided into one of those dusty dreadlock hairstyles confused white people sometimes arrange for themselves.

I was wrong with Fleet. Wrong, wrong, wrong, and I'll admit it and I paid the price for it and wasn't allowed back into Food Carnival for another 9 months, until he quit and took a job delivering for Pizza Plus. So now I can shop at Food Carnival again but if I want a pizza I have to call Dominoes but I understand that everything has its price and I can live with that. People make mistakes.

But Phillip Vincent is no mistake. I knew that right away. I knew it the exact moment I spotted him standing in front of our building, him and his friend, unloading boxes from the back of a car.

My father died 19 years ago and Phillip looks 19. Coincidence, right?

Phillip drives an '89 Celebrity and my father drove a '69 Impala, both Chevy's. Coincidence, right?

Fine, I can live with that.

It was something about the way he lifted a speaker from the back seat, squatting down to support the weight with his legs, that reminded me of the way I'd once seen my father lift a heavy cooler. Phillip bent over and pivoted to a standing position and as he lifted his butt ate the crack of his shorts and he said "HEPP!"

"HEPP!" as if it were the name of a dog he was calling.

He said "HEPP!" and I felt something I can't mistake.

Casey said "Who wouldn't feel something? Here's this hot guy wearing cut-off fatigues and no shirt, what's not to feel?"

But that's sordid and common. This isn't about fatigues. It's about reverence and destiny.

"HEPP!"

It was the first official day of autumn and a pale leaf, rustled by the wind, fell at my feet and shuddered before advancing down the sidewalk to where Phillip stood.

I must have been staring because he said, the first thing he said to me was "Do I know you?"

See, he felt it too.

"Do I know you?"

His friend, a chunky red-faced guy, said something under his breath and they both laughed but I didn't take it personally because, more times than not, people are your friends only because they offer you something you think you need. Take Casey for example: dramatic, whiny, walks with a limp because one leg is shorter than the other—still he refuses to wear an elevated shoe because he thinks it would be too obvious. Yet he was my friend because in his company I felt bold and whole and full of life each time I took note of that fact that, unlike him, I don't dip my shoulders when I walk. I don't bray or overreact.

"Do I know you?"

I said, I was almost speechless, I said "Do you need any help? Can I give you a hand?"

His friend handed me a pillow and said "Knock yourself out." Just then Casey stuck his fat head out of our apartment window and called down "Manny, your mother's on the phone."

Then Phillip gently took the pillow from my hand and said "You'd better go talk to your mother," exactly the way he used to say it. The exact same way.

And that cinched it right there.

On the phone my mother said "I've been thinking," and I thought Well, there's a first time for everything.

"I've been thinking that if you want a knapsack or something for Christmas that now's the time to tell me because there's a sale going on."

And I just shouted "Mother, I'm thirty-three Goddamned years old," and I hung up. A knapsack! My God. Who does she think she's dealing with?

The next evening I went upstairs to Phillip's apartment. I went with a box of fruit turnovers, he always liked turnovers, and a girl answered the door wearing tight pants and a U of M sweat-shirt. She was a sleepy, long-haired, cheap kind of a girl. The girl pushed back her hair with her hands and looked down at the turnovers and said "That's so sweet." Then Phillip walked up and she put her hands on his shoulders and said "Look Phil. Look what he brought us. Aren't people sweet."

Phillip said he guessed they were.

And I was crushed in a way, upset to see my father tangled up with this person. I told Casey what happened and he said "I could have told you the guy was straight."

That perked me up because this isn't about labels. I suppose you could have said that my father was officially "straight," if he'd had to fill in some block on a form. It's just a word choice, and words are nothing at all. Sometimes you just have to throw up your hands in despair and surrender because the words don't exist to describe how you feel.

So maybe he does have some cheap slut of a girlfriend. It's happened before. It won't last.

Casey says no. He says "Face it, Manny. It's a fact." But what is a fact but just another bad four-letter word choice?

Facts are designed out of spitefulness, meant to bully out the privilege of wonder and probability.

Casey's not looking hard enough.

Up close the facts lose their original message. Under examination they become abstract and clouded and open themselves to the mystery and possibility we cannot name to save our lives— only express, as rapture.

———————————————

6

Xavier was a fierce, full-blooded man. Very strong, this guy. Loved the tango. Went to see *The Last Tango in Paris* and got terribly excited. He didn't understand the film: he thought it was a sex movie. He didn't realize it was the story of a desperate man.

The night he saw *The Last Tango in Paris* the three of them went to bed together: Xavier, Carmen, and Beatrice. Everyone knew that Xavier was a bigamist, living with two women.

Every night it was one of them. Sometimes twice a night. The extra one would remain watching. Neither was jealous of the other.

Beatrice ate anything that didn't move: she was fat and dumpy. Carmen was tall and thin.

The night of the last tango in Paris was memorable for the three of them. By dawn they were exhausted. But Carmen got up in the morning, prepared a great breakfast — with heaping spoonfuls of thick condensed milk — and brought it to Beatrice and Xavier. She was groggy with sleep and had to take a cold shower to snap back into shape.

That day — Sunday — they dined at three in the afternoon. Beatrice, the fat one, cooked. Xavier drank French wine. And ate a whole fried chicken by himself. The two women ate the other chicken. The chickens were filled with a stuffing made of raisins and prunes, nice and moist.

At six o'clock the three of them went to church. They seemed a bolero. Ravel's bolero.

That night they stayed home watching television and eating. Nothing happened that night: they all three were very tired.

And so it went, day after day.

Xavier worked hard to support the women and himself, to provide big spreads. And once in a while he would cheat on both of them with a first-rate prostitute. But he didn't say anything about this at home because he was no fool.

Days, months, years went by. Nobody died. Xavier was forty-seven. Carmen thirty-nine. And Beatrice had already turned fifty.

Life was good to them. Sometimes Carmen and Beatrice would go out in order to buy sexy nightgowns. And to buy perfume. Carmen was the more elegant. Beatrice, with her overflowing flesh, would pick out bikini panties and a bra too small for her enormous breasts.

One day Xavier got home quite late at night: the two were desperate. If they had only known that he had been with his prostitute! The three were in truth four, like the Three Musketeers.

Xavier arrived with a bottomless hunger. And opened a bottle of champagne. He was full of energy. He spoke excitedly with the two of them, telling them that the pharmaceutical business which he owned was doing well financially. And he proposed that they go, the three of them, to Montevideo, to stay in a luxury hotel.

In a great hurry-scurry, the three suitcases were packed.

Carmen took all of her complicated make-up. Beatrice went out and bought a miniskirt. They went by plane. They sat down in a row of three seats: he between the two women.

In Montevideo they bought anything they felt like. Even a sewing machine for Beatrice and a typewriter which Carmen wanted so as to be able to learn how to type. Actually she didn't need anything, poor nothing that she was. She kept a diary: she noted down on the pages of a thick, red-bound notebook the dates on which Xavier asked for her. She gave the diary to Beatrice to read.

In Montevideo they bought a book of recipes. Only it was in French, and they understood nothing. The ingredients looked more like dirty words.

Then they bought a recipe book in Spanish. And they did the

best they could with the sauces and the soups. They learned to make "rosbif." Xavier gained seven pounds and his bull-like strength increased.

Sometimes the two women would stretch out on the bed. The day was long. And, although they were not homosexuals, they excited each other and made love. Sad love.

One day they told Xavier about it.

Xavier trembled. And wanted the two of them to make love in front of him that night. But, ordered up like this, it all ended in nothing. The two women cried, and Xavier became furious.

For three days he didn't say a word to them.

But during this period, and without any request, the two women went to bed together and succeeded.

The three didn't go to the theater. They preferred television. Or eating out.

Xavier had bad table manners: he would pick up food with his hands and make a lot of noise chewing, besides eating with his mouth open. Carmen, who was more genteel, would feel revolted and ashamed. But Beatrice was totally shameless, even walking around the house stark naked.

No one knows how it began. But it began.

One day Xavier came home from work with traces of lipstick on his shirt. He couldn't deny that he had been with his favorite prostitute. Carmen and Beatrice each grabbed a piece of wood, and they chased Xavier all over the house. He ran like a madman, shouting "Forgive me, forgive me, forgive me!"

The two women, tired out, finally gave up chasing him.

At three in the morning Xavier wanted to have a woman. He called Beatrice because she was less vindictive. Beatrice, soft and tired, gave herself to the desires of the man who seemed a superman.

But the following day they told him that they wouldn't cook for him anymore. That he'd better work it out with his third woman.

Both of them cried from time to time, and Beatrice made a potato salad for the two of them.

That afternoon they went to the movies. They ate out and

didn't come home until midnight. They found Xavier beaten, sad, and hungry. He tried to explain: "It's just that sometimes I want to do it during the daytime!"

"Well then," said Carmen, "why didn't you come home then?"

He promised he would. And he cried. When he cried, Carmen and Beatrice felt heartbroken. That night the two women made love in front of him, and he ate out his heart with envy.

How did the desire for revenge begin? The two women drew closer all the time and began to despise him.

He did not keep his promise but sought out the prostitute. She really turned him on because she used a lot of dirty language. And called him a son-of-a-bitch. He took it all.

Until there came a certain day.

Or better, a night. Xavier was sleeping placidly, like the good citizen he was. The two women were sitting together at a table, pensive. Each one thought of her lost childhood. And of death. Carmen said:

"One day the three of us will die."

Beatrice answered:

"And for what?"

They had to wait patiently for the day on which they would close their eyes forever. And Xavier? What should be done with Xavier? He looked like a sleeping child.

"Are we going to wait for him to die a natural death?" asked Beatrice.

Carmen thought, thought and said:

"I think we ought to figure something out, the two of us."

"What kind of thing?"

"I don't know yet."

"But we have to decide."

"You can leave it to me, I know what to do."

And nothing was done, nothing at all. In a little while it would be dawn, and nothing had happened. Carmen made good strong coffee for the two of them. And they ate chocolates until they were nauseous. And nothing, nothing at all.

They turned on the portable radio and listened to some poignant Schubert. It was pure piano. Carmen said:

"It has to be today."

Carmen led and Beatrice obeyed. It was a special night: full of stars which looked at them sparkling and tranquil. What silence. But what silence! The two went up close to Xavier to see if it would inspire them. Xavier snorted. Carmen felt really inspired.

She said to Beatrice:

"There are two butcher knives in the kitchen."

"So what?"

"So there are two of us, and we've got two knives."

"So what?"

"So, you ass, we two have arms and can do what we have to do. God directs us."

"Wouldn't it be better not to mention God at this moment?"

"Do you want me to talk about the Devil? No, I speak of God who is the master of all. Of space and time."

Then they went to the kitchen. The two butcher knives were newly sharpened, of fine, polished steel. Would they have the strength?"

They would, yes.

They were armed. The bedroom was dark. They struck blindly, stabbing at the bedclothes. It was a cold night. Then they finally were able to make out the sleeping body of Xavier.

Xavier's rich blood spread across the bed and dripped down onto the floor—a lavish waste. Carmen and Beatrice sat down next to the dining-room table, under the yellow light of the naked bulb, exhausted. To kill requires strength. Human strength. Divine strength. The two were sweaty, silent, knocked out. If it had been possible, they wouldn't have killed their great love.

And now? Now they had to get rid of the body. The body was large. The body was heavy.

So the two women went into the garden and, armed with two shovels, dug a grave in the ground.

And, in the dark of the night, they carried the corpse out into the garden. It was difficult because Xavier dead seemed to weigh more than when he was alive, since his spirit had left him. As they carried him, they groaned from exhaustion and grief. Beatrice cried.

They put the huge corpse in the grave, covered it with the humid and fragrant earth of the garden, earth good for planting. Then they went back into the house, made some more coffee, and pulled themselves together a bit.

Beatrice, great romantic that she was — having filled her life with comic-book romances about crossed or lost love — Beatrice had the idea of planting roses in that fertile soil.

So they went out again to the garden, took a stem of red roses, and planted it on the sepulcher of the lamented Xavier. Day was dawning. The garden gathered dew. The dew was a blessing on the murder. Such were their thoughts, seated on the white bench that was out there.

The days passed. The two women bought black dresses. And scarcely ate. When night came sadness fell over them. They no longer felt like cooking. In a rage, Carmen, the hotheaded one, tore up the book of recipes in French. She kept the one in Spanish: you never know when you might need it again.

Beatrice took over the cooking. They both ate and drank in silence. The stalk of red roses seemed to have taken hold. Good planter's hands, good prosperous earth. Everything was working out.

And so the story would have ended.

But it so happened that Xavier's secretary found his boss's long absence strange. There were important papers to be signed. Since Xavier's house had no telephone, he went there himself. The house seemed bathed in "mala suerte," evil fortune. The two women told him that Xavier had gone on a trip, that he had gone to Montevideo. The secretary didn't much believe them, but behaved as if he swallowed the story.

The following week the secretary went to the police. With the police you don't play games. At first they didn't want to believe his story. But, in the face of the secretary's insistence, they lazily decided to order the polygamist's house searched. All in vain: no trace of Xavier.

Then Carmen spoke:

"Xavier is in the garden."

"In the garden? Doing what?"

"Only God knows."

"But we didn't see anything or anybody."

They went out to the garden: Carmen, Beatrice, the secretary named Albert, two policemen, and two other men whose identities are unknown. Seven people. Then Beatrice, without a tear in her eye, showed them the flowering grave. Three men opened the grave, ruining the stalk of roses, which suffered this human brutality for no reason at all.

And they saw Xavier. He was horrible, deformed, already half eaten away by worms, with his eyes open.

"And now?" said one of the policemen.

"And now we arrest the two women."

"But," said Carmen, "let us be in the same cell."

"Look," said one of the policemen, right in front of the astonished secretary, "it's best to pretend that nothing at all happened, otherwise there will be lots of noise, lots of paper work, lots of gossip."

"You two," said the other policeman, "pack your bags and go and live in Montevideo. And don't bother us anymore."

The two women said thank you very much.

And Xavier didn't say anything. For, in fact, he had nothing to say.

7

It did! It really happened!

Serjoca was a beautician. But he wanted nothing from women. He liked men.

And he did Aurelia Nascimento's make-up. Aurelia was pretty, and made up she became radiant. She was blonde, wore a wig and false eyelashes. They became friends. They went out together, you know, for a meal at a bar, that kind of thing.

Whenever Aurelia wanted to look good, she called up Serjoca. Serjoca himself was good-looking. He was tall and slender.

And so it went. A telephone call and they would agree to meet. She would dress well, outdoing herself. She wore contact lenses. And falsies. Her own breasts were pointed, pretty. She only used falsies because she was small breasted. Her mouth was a red rosebud. Her teeth were large and white.

One day, at six in the evening, just when the traffic was at its worst, Aurelia and Serjoca were standing in front of the Copacabana Palace waiting in vain for a taxi: Serjoca, worn out, was leaning against a tree. Aurelia was impatient. She suggested that they give the doorman ten cruzeiros to get them a cab. Serjoca refused: he was tough when it came to money.

It was almost seven o'clock. It was getting dark. What should they do?

Near them stood Affonso Carvalho. Manufacturer. Industrialist. He was waiting for his chauffeur with the Mercedes. It was hot out, but the car was air conditioned and had a telephone and refrigerator. Affonso had turned forty the day before.

He noticed the impatience of Aurelia, who was tapping her foot on the pavement. An interesting woman, thought Affonso. And she needs a ride. He turned to her:

"Excuse me, are you having some difficulty in finding a taxi?"

"I've been here since six o'clock and not one taxi has stopped for us. I can't take it much longer."

"My chauffeur will be here shortly," said Affonso. "Could I give you two a ride somewhere?"

"I would be most grateful, especially since my feet ache."

But she didn't say that she had corns. She hid the defect. She was fully made up and looked at the man with desire. Serjoca was very quiet.

Finally the chauffeur arrived, got out, and opened the door. The three got in. She in front, next to the chauffeur, the other two in back. She discreetly took off a shoe and sighed with relief.

"Where do you want to go?"

"We don't have anywhere in particular to go," Aurelia said, more and more aroused by Affonso's virile face.

He said: "What if we go to the Number One for a drink?"

"I'd love to," said Aurelia. "Wouldn't you, Serjoca?"

"Sure, I need a strong drink."

So they went to the bar, almost empty at that hour. And they talked. Affonso talked of metallurgy. The other two didn't understand a thing. But they pretended to understand. It was boring. But Affonso was carried away and, under the table, put his foot on top of Aurelia's foot. Precisely the foot with a corn. Excited, she responded. Then Affonso said:

"And what if we were to have dinner at my house? Today I'm having escargots and chicken with truffles. What do you say?"

"I'm starving."

Serjoca said nothing. He too was on fire for Affonso.

The apartment was carpeted in white, and there was a sculpture by Bruno Giorgi. They sat down, had another drink, and went into the dining room. A table of dark rosewood. A waiter serving from the left. Serjoca didn't know how to eat snails and fumbled ineptly with the special silverware. He didn't like it. But Aurelia enjoyed it a lot, even though she was afraid of smelling of garlic.

And they all drank French champagne throughout the meal. No one wanted dessert, they just wanted coffee.

And they went into the living room. There Serjoca came alive. And began to talk as if he'd never stop. He threw languid glances at the businessman, who on his part was surprised at the eloquence of the good-looking young fellow. The next day he would call Aurelia to tell her Serjoca was a lovely person.

And they agreed to meet again. This time at a restaurant, the Albamar. They ate oysters to begin with. Again, Serjoca had trouble eating the oysters. I'm a failure, he thought.

But before they got together, Aurelia had called up Serjoca: she desperately needed to be made up. He went to her house.

Then, while she was being made up, she thought: Serjoca is taking off my face.

It felt as if he were wiping away her features: emptiness, a face merely of flesh. Brown flesh.

She felt ill. She excused herself and went to the bathroom to look at herself in the mirror. It was just as she had imagined: Serjoca had destroyed her face. Even the bones—and she had spectacular bone structure—even the bones had disappeared. He's soaked me up, she thought, he's going to destroy me. And it's on account of Affonso.

She returned dispirited. At the restaurant she scarcely spoke. Affonso spoke mostly with Serjoca, hardly looking at Aurelia: he was interested in the young man.

Finally, finally the luncheon ended.

Serjoca made a date to meet Affonso that night. Aurelia said she couldn't go, that she was tired. It was a lie: she wouldn't go because she didn't have a face to show.

Arriving home, she took a long bubble bath and sat thinking: a little longer and he'll take away my body as well. What could she do to recover what had been hers? Her individuality?

She left the bathroom thoughtfully. She dried herself with an enormous red towel. Thinking the whole time. She weighed herself on the scale: her weight was good. A little longer and he'll take away my weight as well, she thought.

She went to the mirror. She looked at herself for a long time.

But she was nothing anymore.

Then — then, suddenly, she gave herself a hard slap on the left side of her face. To wake up. She stood still, looking at herself. And, as if it hadn't been enough, she gave herself two more slaps. To find herself.

And it really happened!

In the mirror she finally saw a human face. Sad. Delicate. She was Aurelia Nascimento. She had just been born. Nas-ci-men-to.

8

Richard House   Milk

Terry asked me a very simple question yesterday. He asked me if I liked him, because frankly, he said, he didn't think that I did. I told him not to be so stupid. But having thought about it, I don't think that it was such a stupid question. I can't say that I like him. Terry and Simon are my upstairs neighbours. The council gave Terry housing as part of the community plan on account of his sickness. They'd been living there for a good nine months before I met them. It hit both his stomach and his kidneys at the same time. I kept hearing water running through the pipes. Their bathroom pipes go straight through my bedroom. There's nothing I don't hear. I wanted to say something and I've forgotten why I didn't now. But I'm glad I didn't. Well I didn't hear anything for a while until about three, four days later when they brought him home in an ambulance. I must have been out when they took him. Simon said that he should have been in a hospital sooner than he was, but the wards are so dirty they often come back worse than they went in. About a week later Simon comes around, says he doesn't like to ask, he was terribly uncomfortable, but would I mind keeping an eye on Terry. Seems like he couldn't be left on his own. Simon wanted to go and fetch someone. Said he wouldn't be long. It was late, ten-ish. He had to collect someone from the bus, they wouldn't come onto the estate by themselves, seeing as it was dark. That was when I learned that Terry has AIDS. You wouldn't know to look at him. I'd imagine he wasn't ever a handsome man and perhaps he's a little thin, but not so's you'd ever notice. Simon had gone out to fetch Terry's mother, Miriam. Seemingly it was the first time she'd seen him since he'd become sick. He'd suffered depressions when he was younger and she'd looked after him, so Simon thought that it was a good idea to have her stay. I don't think she even stayed the night. So I sat in the sitting room surrounded by Simon's magazines and books and waited. Terry was supposedly asleep in his room. Simon said I virtually ran out of the house when they returned, but it wasn't for what he thought it was. Part of my discomfort about Terry is that he reminds me of my son. I remember Miriam was standing in the doorway, looking very uncomfortable. I just said hello, and good night and squeezed past. There is a sense when something happens to you, a realisation that this is how things are. This is how things really are. There's no getting around it. I had been away for two months, on holiday, convalescing. Visiting my sister in Australia. I was recuperating after an operation to re-attach the tendons in my right knee. They had identified him whilst I was on the flight home, so they were waiting for me at the airport. I was expecting Kenneth to be there, but they took me into a small room even before I could collect my luggage. I wanted him to see me walking, but I wasn't given the chance to get through. They picked me out even before Customs. I was trying to think, have I brought back too much currency? How do they know about the fruit in my bags? Surely it can't be that serious. Kenny wasn't one for waiting long. There's nothing in life that can prepare you for it. There were three policemen and one lady, and a smart gentleman. Even before he explained I could see he was uncomfortable. It must have been an awful job for him. Death is so embarrassing. It had been on the news, even in Australia. So it was somewhere in the back of my head. Afterwards I kept thinking, if they'd just let me walk through Customs it will be alright, that Kenny would be there, waiting. I hated him for telling me. It's your son. I'm very sorry. I'm very sorry. He wasn't sorry at all. He was embarrassed. For a long time afterwards I wanted to die. But you don't do you? You just keep waking up and it's lying there beside you, the first thing to remember. But it wouldn't rest there. Not with the papers and the news, I was on twice a day for nearly a week. The bereaved mother with touching little stories about her son. I told them everything, and when all of the facts came out they twisted every word I said, and they crucified him. They had all of the advantages. I hardly knew what day it was, and they knew exactly what they wanted to hear. They even came out with a book, I wouldn't have anything to do with it at that point. Simon says it's probably just as well. The worst of it was that they called him a whore. Not in so many words of course. And they made me sound stupid, like some babbling imbecile. I kept thinking at the start; what do have I to get up for? What disgusting little detail will I discover today? One thing about it being on the news was that I couldn't exactly hide myself away. Reporters. I had them everywhere. I even found one rummaging through my trash. It was something like two in the morning. I was very polite. I asked him who he was and what he thought he was doing. He just outright said that if I was at all interested in who had murdered Kenneth that I should let him in the house. He wanted to see his room and look through his drawers. I nearly let him in. I canceled all of my papers of course. I have found that there is little point in trying to reason to people who are shameless. Simon and Terry were on a TV special. After it aired for the first time, some reporters came round to interview them in the flats. Terry refused to get dressed and stood as bare as the day he was born at the front door and asked them, well, isn't this what you came for? Isn't this human interest? I laughed till I cried when Simon told me. Terry used such bad language that they couldn't use any of it. Simon's just happy that he wasn't so difficult when they filmed the special. Terry was on a tear afterwards; what do you think they were here for, to ask me about my life? It isn't life that they are interested in. He has a point there. It became something marvelous. In his own way Kenny told them everything, except for a name. They knew everything except the identity of who murdered him. They knew his sex, weight, hair colour, that he was left-handed. They could even tell which of the blows came first. They had it all planned out somewhere, choreographed like a dance. I had never considered it. I mean you use a fork, an ordinary kitchen fork all of the time. It's something you eat with every day of your life. It was a measure of his sickness to me that he had the imagination, if you can even call it that, to use a simple innocent household fork. Innocent is such a strange word. I never thought of Kenny as innocent. He'd had plenty of friends, plenty of men friends, so he wasn't naive. Sometimes, if there was anyone special, I'd meet them at work if they came to pick him up. But we never discussed it. I got him his first proper job, and we worked together for a while, at the D.O.E. Despite what the papers thought, I did know the kind of company that Kenny kept, but I had no idea that he was keeping another apartment, I would never have guessed. There was no reason to. Everything became so public. Working together I knew everything, or thought I did. I knew exactly what his wage was, so it never would have occurred to me that he could afford another place, or that he'd want one. But then I forget that there was other money coming in for him; or as the police put it, money from his friend. Friend. Funny how that word covers such a lot of ground these days. I didn't have a clue really. That was especially hard. They wouldn't release the body. He'd had a boyfriend I'd never met and they were certain that it was him, and they were after him, they said, for eighteen months. Never found him of course. They kept the body for over eighteen months before we could bury him. I was on the telly for that as well. I didn't think that it was the boyfriend, I just wanted him to come forward. I didn't start eating right until I moved. Kenny did most of the cooking, and I couldn't face the kitchen. I had to learn everything over again, eating, cooking, how to spend time on my own. Everything had to be re-learned. Simon says the same thing about Terry. He never realised how much he took for granted. Even how he talks to Terry. Do you realise how much we talk about death? Simon says he feels like he's constantly throwing his health in Terry's face. Terry and I very rarely talk, yet I see him just about every day. I don't generally leave for work until about eleven-thirty, as they've cut my hours. It was either that or switch to two and a half days. The last thing I do before work is to give Terry his drink. It's basically warm milk and malt, and some vegetable protein that Simon brings me. Sometimes, more frequently now, Simon will stay overnight so he will answer the door, then I'll stay and chat. If it's Terry it usually means that I've woken him up so I just hand him the drink and leave. On the odd occasion he'll hide behind the door, and I know he's not decent. If Simon can't be there, and Terry has a doctor's appointment I'll wake him up earlier, unless I hear the pipes, then I know he's up. They never come round in the afternoon, which wasn't so good in the beginning, but Terry will sleep at any opportunity now. Dr. Gilbert, or Giblets as Terry calls him. Terry has only spoken to me once about when he was diagnosed. He said he had waited a long time, believing that everything would just go away. There wasn't any one particular thing troubling him, more like a number of problems. He was referred to Dr. Gilbert directly. After Dr. Gilbert gave him the results of his tests, Terry said that he apologised to the doctor, he said he just couldn't comprehend it. Who ever did it, and I doubt if they will ever find out now, I think I have forgiven. You feel like you never will. You just want them to suffer. I think you can feel too much in life. That you can weary of it, simply run out of it. You find you simply have no hate left in you. I have no curiosity. I can't say I'm happy, or as happy as I used to be. But then I can't say I'm unhappy either. Simon says that you can't close a life, even death doesn't do that. You can dispose of the body, but there's always memory. He doesn't know the first thing about it. Memory is as corruptible as flesh. Whenever I try and picture Kenny, I get the photograph that the papers used, one we'd taken years ago in our first flat. I can remember the picture being taken. I mean I know it was because I was there, but the only picture I get in my head, is the photograph the papers used, exactly as it was. They'd cut out his father and me and just used his face. You could almost make out the dots of his smile, but it was so grainy and blurred. It's a nice sentiment though. That was a lie a little earlier, when I said that I didn't know he wanted his own place, well, that was a lie. We'd actually spoken a few times about Kenneth getting a place of his own. Though I doubt now if we both had the same idea in mind. I'm not saying the place was a palace, but it was home, our home, a home that had stayed intact even through a war, several in fact if you count the smaller ones. As it turned out it just wasn't practical, not until I'd had my knee done at least. I needed him for everything, lifting packages, everything. I couldn't even make the bed. He said that he could come round regularly; see to my laundry and cleaning. But I said, what if I fell again or if I needed something in the middle of the night? I couldn't manoeuvre around so well. I needed someone to help me dress in the mornings, someone to help me into the bathroom. When your knee goes you're completely stuck. Everything we do has some amount of bending or twisting, and it was so painful. I was lucky really, they changed my job to Inventory. So I could still work and I had a desk for the first time in my life. And there was always Kenny. I can't say they didn't do their job. The police that is. Though I could never have accused them of being over-zealous. And I still can't see why they kept the body for so long. They wouldn't say anything other than they were looking for the boyfriend. The boyfriend? They didn't even find out his name. How can you find someone if you don't know who it is you're looking for, I say. I wouldn't go to the place they'd found him. At first they didn't realise that the apartment was his. I wouldn't go. It was a place he'd never wanted me in. I couldn't make myself. I read in the papers that he had had a dog, and that it had been impounded. They said that I had had it destroyed. I called the Police Station to see if it was true. To see if there ever was a dog. I didn't get a clear answer on that one. That was when I decided not to go. I had them deliver his things straight to Oxfam, I didn't want anything to do with them. Turned out that he'd bought all sorts of things, furniture, a bed. They gave me an itemised list, and a thank you note from Oxfam. For a while I regretted my decision. The police told me that it would all make sense, if I just saw the place, that it wasn't the horrid little bed-sit that the papers had made it out to be, but that it was a nice three-room flat. But why should I have gone? Only to be insulted again. He was always so willful. A strange little boy who never ran for hugs. Perhaps something amongst all of this shame would make him laugh. I don't know. I honestly don't know. I had to move in the end. I was seriously thinking of Australia. I couldn't stay in the same house. Thanks to the newspapers everyone knew about Kenneth, every little detail. The council wouldn't have it, of course, said the old place would do just fine, virtually telling me that I didn't know which side my bread was buttered. But I didn't want him hanging over my shoulder, not the new Kenneth. It was like I kept breathing the same air, slowing myself down. I had two years of public ridicule and vilification at the hands of the British press after the death of my son. It left me wanting to firmly close some doors and move on. So I had a word with the M.P. who'd petitioned for the release of the body. I didn't want to do it, but it did the job. Within two months I had a nice place overlooking Ladywell Park. He even made them pay for the move. I was glad to leave Peckham. This summer it will have been seven years. I had to change my job of course. I do miss some things about the D.O.E., mostly the journey there, waiting for Kenny, the crush of the trains, both of which always made me cross. The buses were too slow of course. Then there was the walk, either down Victoria, or along the Thames from Waterloo. Now I just hop on a number 19, and I'm there in five minutes. I'm at the D.E. now, nice people, local office, but not the same sense of importance. And now I have to pack a lunch, I miss the canteen. I hadn't realized until I watched the TV special, but Simon isn't Terry's partner. I thought that it was a little funny, all the comings and goings, and at all hours. There's three of them all together, Simon, Terry and the nurse. Simon only does for Terry, didn't even know Terry before he was sick. He's a volunteer. He calls me Lill, or Lilly, I don't mind which. I've never been a Lillian. Kenny went by everything, our Ken, Kenneth, he didn't care much for Kenny though. The nurse is generally only there twice a week, more if they need. But Simon is a blessing, he's happy to help out now and then, just with the little things though. I tell you I wouldn't mind putting my feet up once in a while and having someone do for me all day what that Simon does for Terry. About a week ago I had a visitor. I told Simon about it, apparently a similar thing had happened to them, a short while after their special. Someone came round to their door, saying that they were part of a group petitioning the release of new drugs. Sounded very well organized, and that having seen Terry's story on the telly, and for a small fee they could supply him with a newsletter about new drugs and testing and such, and they'd also be contributing to a charity. Simon gave him five on the spot. Said that he would have given more if he had had it, he was so convinced. That was the same day someone sprayed something on their door. Simon wouldn't say what the word was. They haven't yet seen a newsletter. Lord knows how they found the address. Simon thinks that they live locally. He said that there are some very sad and pathetic individuals who feed off others' grief, and that'd be what my visitor was about. He made more out of it than there actually was. My visitor wanted me to join a dating service for senior singles. He wanted eighty pounds. I told him I didn't see why anybody should have to pay for company, and that if I wanted the kind of company that they were offering, well, I think I could manage that by myself. Simon said I should be careful for a while in case he was just checking the house to see if there was someone else around. I shouldn't have let him know that I was single. He's right of course. I gave Simon a key and asked him to keep an eye out and look in on me whenever he has a chance, you never know now do you? I asked Simon if he thought that Terry had been reckless, and he said no, how can you be reckless when you don't even know what's at stake. He understood completely. Said no, but he understood. He said once you start making judgments like that you're not a hundred miles from blaming someone. He said that people often proscribe something as dangerous when they either don't like it or don't understand it. So you have to sift through all of this nonsense and find out for yourself. He said it's a common attitude to think, well, they got what was coming to them. He said he understood how I could blame Kenny, which I've never actually said to him. But he couldn't blame Terry. Then after he'd thought for a while he said, well perhaps it isn't that different after all, because Kenneth didn't ask to be killed. I was angry with him and wouldn't see him for a while. I was thinking of asking for my keys back, because in his own way he had said that Terry was better than Kenny because Terry was somehow innocent. He came and apologised. Said he wasn't sure what he'd said, but that he was sorry. Simon also told me that when he was younger he used to walk up by the lights at the by-pass. And if he saw anyone interesting he'd wave at them and stop them, and get into the car with them. He said he understands more now what he was up to, and that he wouldn't do it again, though not because he didn't want to either. You can't be sure of anyone these days, he said. I can't imagine it myself. He said that if there was any reason to this thing, then he'd be dead too. Says we probably don't know the half of it. I had thought that Simon was a little more sensible. I don't like to think that they all behave like that. I've only recently returned to church. Not the same one of course. It's a comfort of sorts, even though I'm not sure that I need it anymore. I found it irritating that people could offer you sympathy when they obviously don't have a clue. Anglicans can be so particular, snobbish. You name it and people can be selfish with it, that's what Simon says. He doesn't like me going to church, makes fun of it. But I tell him, you should try it, the both of you, if nothing else the services are aerobic, all that kneeling might do some good. Plus the vicar isn't bad looking. When the service is over I could almost give out a little cheer, it's like running laps with your breath held. It's not even as if I believe. Where was He for Kenneth? That's what I say, and what's He going to do about Terry and all those others like him? I watched a programme two nights ago about the American Civil War, and at the end, there was a story about a steamship returning hundreds of soldiers home, after years of fighting. The boiler exploded and all of them died. Hundreds of them. Where was He then? You'd imagine after years of terrible, terrible war you'd be allowed some peace. But that's not how things work out is it? I'd like to ask the vicar, but he hasn't any experience of it, you can tell. Besides they always say you shouldn't question Him, that everything has a purpose even famine. That's just an excuse of course, anyone can see through that. How can there be a reason for being stabbed to death with a kitchen fork? Simon says that if you don't get what you need, within reason, then you shouldn't pay for it in taxes. I've given it a lot of thought, and it makes sense. I mean Simon is voluntary. Nobody pays him? If it wasn't for his compassion, and others like him, Terry might as well be on that steamboat too, just waiting for the boiler to blow. I think they should take out what they need from their own taxes. Simon is registered as unemployed and they keep badgering him for a job. If the D.H.S.S. knew how much time he spent with Terry they would penalize him for being unavailable for work. They would cut his benefit because he is technically employed. I say they should pay him, or provide an optional service for Terry. Not that they're ever likely to. What use to Terry is a nurse once or twice a week? They should demand more, it stands to reason. They should demand much more. Working with Government has taught me one thing, they do listen, they have to. Politicians are terrified of anyone with a loud voice, especially if they are making sense. Simon subscribes to the conspiracy theory. Just about everything is a conspiracy it seems. Organised religion, Terry's illness, Kenneth's death, and their refusal to release the body. But it doesn't stop there, he thinks that TV, and radio are conspiracies. Bad programming is definitely a conspiracy, he might be right there. You wouldn't believe half of the nonsense I watch. Even the post. He says he writes every day but seldom gets a response. Says someone is keeping an eye on them, reads their post. I don't know what I think. Simon bought a video player for Terry's birthday. Dropped off the back of a truck he said, just so Terry wouldn't feel funny about the money. We all chipped in of course. Despite herself Terry's mother came up with the lion's share. Still, she didn't come. You do realise that I have other children, I can't let his disease run my life, she said. I think that she should accept more responsibility for the way Terry is and all. Terry cooked us something spicy, Indian I think. I thought the purpose of all of those spices was to disguise the taste of rancid meat. Terry's quite a master in the kitchen it seems. He couldn't eat any of it, he just wanted to cook for us. Simon tried to dissuade him, but he wouldn't have any of it. Spicy food's hard for his stomach, being temperamental. The smell of the fats and spices alone were enough to set him off, and that was that for Terry. So Simon cleaned up and made sandwiches, and we watched the special again, only with the sound turned down. Simon can't stand his voice, and we whisked past the hospital scenes. I can't watch injections, never could, it turns my stomach. Simon warned me, don't watch Lilly, he said, don't watch. All that was left was pictures of them both walking through Greenwich Park, which they don't usually do. Funnily enough I remember Simon catching a cold, they kept them out there so long till they got what they wanted. Seeing the Centre in the special gave me the idea of becoming involved, and Simon was very encouraging. I try to be here twice a week, Tuesday and Thursday evenings, for Terry's support group. Terry's mother, Miriam, has started coming too. She's a difficult woman. Hard, very hard. I tell Simon that she probably doesn't mean to be, perhaps you have to lose somebody close before you realise just how precious time can be. So last night was Terry's little show-down. Simon called it a hiccup. Terry asked me why I came, why I bothered to come to the Centre. I was flabbergasted, I didn't know what to say. He says he has a very strong feeling that I don't actually like him. What could I say? There I was on the spot. Simon was just about to say something when Miriam started clapping. Nice, she said. Very nice Terry. So she stands up, pulls on her gloves and says, so let's try again next week shall we? Don't think I can quite make Tuesday. And let's see if we can't be nice? The group leader, Alan, asks her to sit down, says, I don't want to prevent you from leaving but we might follow this through. Then Terry throws up his hands and says, what's the use? Really, what's the point in meeting next week, next month, whenever? Well the upshot of it is, is that Terry was upset about an item on the news. Seemingly there's a new drug which prevents all of your white cells from rushing to your lungs when there's an infection. Apparently this is necessary because all those white cells hamper another drug from dealing with the infection. The doctors who discovered this new drug didn't release it for about six months. They had it, but they didn't release it. Not until they could get the publicity they wanted. As it happens, that drug would have been useful to Terry. Do you realise how many people have died in the six months that they delayed in releasing that drug? There's no doubt in my mind that it's murder, he said. That realisation pretty much shut everyone up again. Then he chirps up once more with, I still say you don't like me. Without thinking I just told him to shut up. When he had first said that a thought rushed through my mind, which was, yes, you're right, I don't like you much at all. And without a doubt some of the things you stand for disgust me. But I think what is happening to you is wrong. It's cruel and it's wrong and I won't turn my back, however mean you are, or however much I dislike you. Thinking about it now I was just excusing myself. If I'm being honest then I have to admit that I'm frankly appalled by Terry. There I've said it. Every time I look at him I think of sex. It's the same with Kenny. I can't get past it. I saw Terry today on the balcony. Gave me a timid little wave. I thought wave all you like you little bugger but you're still owing an apology. It was twelve o'clock and he was standing on the balcony in a bathrobe, and I thought, yes, and a change of attitude wouldn't hurt. So last night I lay in bed wanting to clear my head of everything I'd been thinking about. Mostly Terry, I suppose. I just wish there was something to stop me thinking. If somebody came up to me tomorrow and held out their hand with a pill and said, here, if you take this pill it will all go away, Terry, Kenneth, everything. You'll forget it all. Without a doubt I'd take it. I'm just exhausted thinking about it all. I don't think Terry drinks his milk. I don't know for sure, but Dr. Gilbert has him on a strict diet, and he has a very poor appetite. But I will be there tomorrow, and the next day, eleven o'clock, with his milk. I want him to understand that although I cannot prevent his current suffering, I will not accept that it is reasonable, and I will not accept such loss in my world. Such loss should never be accepted. I've gone over the last months with Kenneth time and time again, and I wonder what might have happened if I had let him have his own place, and if I had known about his boyfriend. I also wonder what else he was dishonest to me about. I don't think that what he did was wrong, necessarily. And it's a hard enough world anyway for me to even pass judgment upon him. He was my son after all, and you have to love your own kind, don't you? I can't even say that he was looking out for trouble either. Lord knows it's hard enough. Even without asking for it you get it. I try not to watch the news too much because I always think, that's another one, perhaps he's killed again. Somebody else's son. Somebody else's child. And the panic just won't leave me. If I could make it all go away, if I could make it all stop tomorrow then I would. Because I don't see us dealing with half of the problems we have in this world whilst we're up to our necks in them. And the more I think about it, the more it frightens me. I'd just appreciate some distance. I mean

how can we deal with the specifics when we don't even have a
wider picture?

9

Patricia's gray hair was like wire mesh: when she pushed it back, it stuck brittlely in place. Joe called her eyes little blue birds. Silence was all around her mind. Her years were not quiet because he talked and talked, but his words had slowly become unspecific like a hum in a field. He poured gin into himself the way ground takes rain. When he fell flat dead asleep, she pulled him to bed, removed his shoes. He was a trapped man and cried because of it. In the mornings he held her tightly and rubbed his calloused hand through her hair. He called her 'urchin'. "You're my only honey," he'd say. "I still love you."

Their home was small and dark. Joe liked to sit at the kitchen table with its red and white checkered tablecloth. There were two chairs and one window to look out of. He said he needed her to be there. She had become distracted, did not wash the dishes, sweep or move much. Her heart had shrunk into a tiny pebble and lay small and still. She thought: *he's eating himself*. But there was never a time to say this.

He would come home from work and slap his hat down, "Christ, ten years of the same crap. Patty come over here. Rub my back. They're breaking my bones. You know what construction makes you? A spineless slug, honey. They're hiring cheap young kids. But don't you worry; I'm making it so they can't afford to can me. Just appreciate that. Look at you—Christ you're fat. What are you: four hundred pounds? I'm ashamed to take you out."

He did not mean what he said to her. He bought her presents, said: "Don't mention it." Once, it was a boxed set of five ball-point pens, with only three in it. The plastic box was new and it said "5." All evening, she worried about the disappeared pens. Tears began to slip out of her eyes. "Christ, there's never anything happy about you," Joe said. She bowed her head: tears plopped on the plastic and began to run off in little lines. "Oh, honey," Joe said. "It's OK. Don't I know it's a damned bad life."

His hands were large and heavy and, the third time he beat her, he broke her jaw so that they had to tie it up with wires at the hospital. They told her that because some bone chips had already slivered loose from another time, this was the last occasion she'd have to heal properly. The doctor said, "A jaw is sufficiently frail; you'd better think you need it."

They didn't allow Joe to visit her and the room was quiet, very white. There were moments when she heard people in the other rooms breathe in a strained way. She ate through straws. The nurses gave Patricia pads of paper. They had handed her magazines with photographs of battered women. Patricia hid them under her bed. The sunlight swept in on her sheets.

Patricia thought of momma's home with its clean flowered curtains and scrubbed surfaces, and momma wearing frilled aprons, brewing jams. The house smelled of baking. Her sheets were hung out to dry in the wind so her beds smelled sweet. Patricia had stumbled meekly through this home full of things momma was bringing to life. Momma ran after her, trying to fix her up. She'd say, "Heavens, take that dress off. I won't have you going around like a wrinkled-up rag. You have got to learn to be more feminine. Patty, there's no man who likes carelessness in a woman." Momma would iron, sweating.

Joe had been muscular, enthusiastic, and he had swept her out of momma's house, seeming not to notice what Patricia could not do. Now they lived in a small dark hole. His thirst chewed him up. Once, while he talked, she noticed long dust balls hanging from the ceiling. She wondered how they had flown up. Momma had never known that houses could become strange.

The nurses bustled through her bright room and looked at her with flat sympathetic eyes. Patricia wondered what was in their hearts. It scared her that they had said this was a last chance. She liked seeing the emerald summer trees out her window and the sky like a sapphire. She drew on her pads and wrote about what she noticed. Women counselors had come to talk to her. They said: "*Why* do you *let* him do it? Ask yourself what your *motivations* are. The *law* is on your side." They spoke about separation, independence, oppression of women. The hum began in her head. "Write what you feel," they said. She wrote: *My husband always makes me listen to him. Please don't talk to me so much.*

They did not come back and she was not sorry because she had not learned anything.

It was a short stay. Joe came to pick her up. "Honey, baby, I missed you so," he said. "I'm a mean sonofabitch but I love you, Pat. I'm just all wrong. You've got to forgive me please, Patty." He gripped the steering wheel in his large reddened hands. Black lines ran through the knuckles and fingertips, making her think about how many divisions skin has. Then she thought about the wires that pulled her jaw together. She wanted to sleep on the thin bed in the guest room. She took out one of the pads they had given her at the hospital and wrote:

Joey, I am very tired.

"I can't read while I'm driving," he said.

There were fewer fat summer trees as Joe neared the house. Frantic yellow grasses filled the horizon, whispering against the doors of the pick-up as it hit the narrow dirt road. The kitchen light was on and the house was spic and span. "I can't believe you're going to have to write notes," Joe said. She wrote:

Joe I have to sleep alone. They're scared about my jaw.

He looked at it. "Did they talk to you funny over there?" he asked. "Hey look, I apologized. Those damned people don't have any rights to tell you where to sleep." But he let her sleep there. His eyes were peculiar, needy.

She stepped through the things thrown and scattered on the floor, cleared the bed and wrapped on clean sheets. That night she dreamed of emerald hills and willow trees and of trying to describe them. When she woke, she felt different, thinking that perhaps finding the right words to draw a picture of something made you see it better and love what you saw — even trees, normal things. If you thought about the particular ways there were to say things maybe you'd care more about all you said and heard. She saw a new hope for her and Joe and she tried to write this to him. He thought her eccentric, thought they had drugged her at the hospital. He checked the vitamin capsules and protein powders the nurses had given her, and he disliked them.

"If they put anything in you, I'll kill them," he said. "And you better sharpen up honey, or I'm dumping this vegetarian shit in the garbage hole."

Patricia wrote frantically:

Joe, if I don't have those I'll die.

She shook it at him. A little hand seemed to grip her heart. "Yes-sir," Joe said. "The way I hear it, you're going to die if you don't get to sleep in that room, too."

Patricia was losing weight. Loose folds came on her throat and legs. Joe threw one of her pads away. Her body was shriveling up. Her heart would shrink. Then her words would fly away: her mind would remain only a hum. She began scavenging for paper and hid pieces in a drawer which, every morning, as soon as Joe left for work, she'd write and write on — about parts of the house, space, individual crickets, grasses. She uncovered terrible complex detail: weeds thinner than skin, baby crickets' eyes. She hid her notes. Joe would come home, pour himself a gin. She saw it running in the lining of his stomach, a chewing stream.

"Patricia, you've got to get out of that room," he said. "You're getting lonely and peculiar."

She wrote:

Joe, it's a last chance. If my jaw doesn't fix up I won't be able to talk again. That's why I have to stay there.

He threw the note on the floor. "Listen," he said. "I can't stand this. You got me kow-towing to some special interpretation and private room business and the hell if I see you doing anything. Didn't they give you some deaf-and-dumb exercises to do? Hell, I bet they did. Now you get yourself practicing or I'm going to knock the damned words into you and not the way you like."

She jumped up from her chair. "Oh, honey," he said. "I didn't mean that. I swear, baby, I'll never hit you again. Oh honey, honey,

I didn't mean to scare you."

The next evening he brought her a present in a crumpled brown bag. Inside, there were colored hair ribbons marked with small black stains. "You don't have to say anything," Joe said. "You deserve them." He drank some gin. "Honey, I'm damned tired," he murmured. "But I do it for you, and for us. I'm bringing in the money. Those vitamin plasters cost a mint, but we manage, right? Now, you should start taking care of yourself so you don't keep shriveling up like a deflated balloon. The thing to do is get exercise."

It became night as he talked. She could see two stars through the window. She was thinking about how big the heavens were outside, how she and Joe never looked out, and Joe's words became a drone. His face turned redder every night. Patricia thought they were sad there, and that she did not hate him, even when he hit her, and that she did not know how to make a change.

(From where Joe sat he didn't have much choice but to contemplate her immovable jaw, squat wired up like a crate. A man had to look at a lot of things he couldn't stand. You might try to talk to people about it, but people had holes in their heads where their ears were supposed to be. The whole damn thing chewed you up. He tried to get it out of his system, talked, told Patty, but she didn't pull it out; she was always across the table, never nearer. What did she want out of him? She had a kind of space in her head — or maybe it was like a wad of cotton, something kind of thick and soft and lost. He had thought he liked that, but it made him sad, and sometimes crazy. It made him wild how people had holes for their ears and they let your words rush out of their minds. He clutched his gin. Then he hated her, wept inside for hating.)

His fists pounded the table. Her head — her eyelids slowly shuttering — had kept snapping to her chest. Suddenly she leapt in the chair, and stared at him, disoriented. "Oh, get the hell to bed," he said.

He lit the fireplace and murmured at the flames. His sweat

poured. His head would fall against his shoulder, sullen and knocked out, soon. Early on, she had used to grow frantic, imagining the house blazing in a terrible pyre. But he would always catch her if she snuck in to put it out. One time he had bought a banjo. She crept in at dawn. He opened one eye. "Honey, I'll play you 'Oh Susanna'," he said quickly, "Jesus, this is a happy song." Once he caught her, she wasn't allowed to leave.

Joe refused to read any more notes, tossed them numerously to the floor. One evening, she wrote:

I want you to die.

He crumpled it. And when he talked she began writing more and more notes, thinking of all the things she felt, and they littered the floor.

When they took her wires out, Joe wanted her to move back into the bedroom. She was thinking of how she sat on the steps outside, in the mornings, looking at the grasses, the way heat made little flies jump, and there were lost little flowers between them. Things she didn't know she knew were coming together. She remembered words from her mother, a tree she used to climb on, and how white the hospital was like snow. She wanted her room.

When Joe slept with her, he called out strange words: wee-zoo, give us a lick, flap it up, baby go. She shut her eyes. He pushed and she felt she had to do it, and she was an animal like a dog or a pig. Before touching her, he would say, "It makes me sad we can't have a baby." Sometimes he did it two or three times. "Maybe you're a little fertile yet," he said. But she was unable to have children. She imagined babies in her, wanted them, to stop him.

In the hospital, she had begun getting strange heats. They examined her, expecting to diagnose an internal hurt, but they found she had started menopause.

Joe said, "Well, it'll be nice to have something warm in bed again. Thin as you are, you'll do. We'll get you fattened up."

She picked up a pad and began writing on it.

"You can talk now, damn it," he said.

She wrote:

I have menopause. I want to sleep in the guest room.

He threw it down. "I don't have to read any damned notes," he said.

She lifted it and smiled at him.

"For Chrissake, what the hell's the matter with you?" Joe said. "Patricia it's over. You're OK."

He read the note. "My God, I don't care about that. Happens to every woman. Honey, don't let that bother you." She wanted her room. She touched her jaw. He jumped up from his chair. "Listen, you're making me crazy," he said.

Patricia started to write a note. She felt she could make him listen. Suddenly, he slapped her.

She ran into her room and turned the key. Her cheek burned. Her jaw was a hot liquid. His sweat, his weight, it would smash and break her up like pieces of clay. When he had shattered her jaw, two teeth had broken, and the blood had come out snaking and spitting on the floor. He screamed, "My God, Patricia." But he didn't remember. He hit, hit. Patricia picked up Joe's pellet gun, thrown in the room long ago and forgotten. She inserted a pellet. She gathered all her papers and put them in her coat pocket. She took the money order. Joe had told momma that Patricia had tripped on the pick-up step and broken her jaw and they needed help with the hospital bills. When the money order had come, Patricia had hidden it with her papers. Joe shook the door.

"Damn bitch," he shouted.

His fist splintered the wood panel; his fingers wriggled through. They were pink, blind worms. They reached for the lock. Her heart beat hard. She lifted the gun. She had to be a warrior. Oh, how was it happening? Joe smashed in; she shot at his face, his hand clutched his forehead, he stumbled and fell. She ran out.

As she ran, she felt how awkward and brittle her body had become, her legs like pitch forks. Joe always left his keys in the pick-up. She turned them in the lock. The engine started. She drove. The pick-up shook on the dirt road. No neighbors would see. There were none. She reached asphalt; everything shouted in her ears: how she had always been fat, with no friends, and no babies, a shame to a husband and, worse now, transformed. She pushed on the accelerator. She wanted to touch her face. The car was going deeper and deeper into fields, dark in the night. She began to cry. And, after that, she felt something was being drawn from her. The car window was open. The wind grabbed at her. It pulled her hair apart. It was whirring things out of her. She felt alone.

In no time, pink climbed up everywhere, and all the grasses were cherry-color sticks, then rosy ones, ruffled up by ground winds. She saw that she was soft and pink, too, through the windshield, and felt that a prettiness had come to protect her, and she began to think about protection. She drove far into a dirt road and stopped the pick-up. Her jaw was OK, didn't hurt anymore. Placing her papers under her head, she lay down. She understood that she needed to get new license plates, a new residence state.

Crickets jumped and rasped all around her truck. She leapt up: she had seen an eye bleeding, then Joe's face. He picked the wet eye out of his head and handed it to her.

The sun was brilliant, burning color out of the sky. The land was flat. Millions of insects flickered from the grasses. She was going out of her mind with thirst, and her hunger became dizziness. She started the pick-up. She had driven in contrary directions, zig-zagging. Following signs, she realized she was near South Dakota. She recognized town names she had heard once or twice. She thought about how words changed, and became necessary places.

The farther she went, the more impossible it seemed for her to go back. She heard people call her criminal, saw how she had been gentle but had finished that. The pick-up surrounded her like a shield. She drove through ten towns afraid of stopping where there were waitresses with their hawk eyes and their plans to help the police. Her muscles and joints ached and her throat was a burning skillet. She wanted to find the words for all this, the things to write. She had to record the hills, where they rose up, and how the horizon yawned like a huge window. The road became a spool of black yarn and unwound where the sky was turning silver, heated. Then different species of birds cried in fields around curves from one another as if the fields were separate countries. Some puffed out of blue and purple breasts, another type flew on slender green feathers like leaves. And, in her sleep, she had nightmares of Joe. If she wrote them down, they might leave her.

In White Owl, she saw a laundromat. It was shady, blue inside, empty with many blue chairs. She parked. She found the bathroom, combed her hair, washed her face, and drank for a long time from the sink. She pulled out her paper and a pen and sat near the washing machines to write. It was very quiet. She scribbled out her harsh dreams, sweating. The road was dusty and sunlit. It was about noon; no one passed outside the laundromat windows.

"Most people have their own washing machines," a dry voice said at her neck. Patricia clutched her paper. "But you don't have money for one." He laughed.

He was extremely thin, old, with many creases in his skin. Red blood vessels sprinkled through his cheekbones. Green veins ran up his temples, into his hair. He leaned a hand on her shoulder and she leapt up. "My God, I'm sorry, " he said. "Nobody's afraid of me here."

She pulled her papers to herself, heading for her pick-up, but he came after her saying he was sorry again and again, asking her, please, to sit. He gave her two donuts and a coffee, and tried to understand what upset her. She shook her head and ate slowly. He began telling her things.

"I got a long life, sweetie. I've been running this quarter and dimes place since I don't know when. At least it's mine, a hell of a lot better than what I tangled myself up with for my hare-brained nephew. He's got me collecting rent from houses I have to drive twenty miles into the middle of nothing to get to. All sorts of people come down that black road, needing a place to stay. You bet you they're beating it back the way they came from after two months. Honey, humanity is fleeing. What are we all going to do if we've got nothing to stick to?"

He said he had half a mind to wish his nephew's places would burn down. Leave little black smudges in the grasses and be done for. Amen. He'd have his peace. "I'm sorry, hon, about how I upset you before. I guess a man doesn't really have a right to go around touching other people, especially these days." Then he looked at her paper. "A letter?" he asked. She shook her head. "You writing love poems?" He winked at her. "Hell, I used to write poetry. It's a good thing to do."

He wore a baseball hat. His eyes were wide, pale, with minuscule veins cross-hatching the whites, gentle and preoccupied. She was thinking of the dream she'd been writing out. Joe had a hole in his head; he had just come back from the hospital where they had bandaged him up and tried to understand if he could think because all he kept crying, with fat tears falling on his shirt, was: "I wanted a baby, a tiny baby." They sent him home; he had to walk for miles. He sat in front of the fire, at home, watching the flames grow and be born from new twigs. Then it grew out of the fireplace, and he was happy because he liked it fertile. And it climbed onto his slippers and set his feet on fire. Joe could not get up. Patricia was shouting, "Water, Water!" but her feet were locked into the floor. Pages of her writing began floating in the air, multiplying, covering her view of him. Then he picked up his drink and threw it on the fire and it burst like an oil refinery. She saw fire shooting out of Joe's head. Patricia's hand was shaking. She spilled some coffee.

"You're sick, honey. You're very sick," the man said. "What's the matter?"

She looked sadly at the thin man. "The dreams will eat me. They're going to get revenge. They make him bleed," she said.

"You talk like a poet," he said. "You got to watch out not to get ill. It's a mean world. Don't you have a family, honey?"

"I can't have babies," Patricia said. "I need a home." She watched his expression with caution but he kept mild. She murmured, "I don't like houses on a road. I would like a place to write, and I can pay."

"Maybe you can write about my laundromat. Would you like that? Hon, I've got a nice place for one person. I'll take you there. Now my name is Frank. You know what I'm going to call you? Pretty Eyes. How do you like that?"

They drove for awhile and reached a green house, all by itself. Frank opened the main door. On the ground floor, to the right, was another door. "Your neighbors," Frank said. "But not for long. They've got the itch, too; they'll be going to Florida. Maybe nobody's got grandchildren. You think that's it?" Short green steps led to a landing with two doors. "OK, this one here is your private bathroom, and this one's your apartment," Frank said.

Patricia liked having two doors, two small places. The apartment was narrow, with a kitchenette at one end. The floors had broad wood panels and the wallpaper was flowered with pink and yellow roses on thorny stems which were gray and jagged. Each rose had five leaves. There was a bed without sheets. The windows stared out to a space of fields. "Momma sent me a check, but I have to change it first," Patricia said.

"Oh, sure honey. You come to the laundromat and pay me. You come and do your laundry for free, too. I've heard about artists falling on hard times."

Patricia thought about how funny people's heads were; what they planted in them. Some sprouted lovely wild blossoms. Others grew mean.

(Joe had lain with his head sunk on the broad-paneled floor for some time after he opened his eyes, his mind anchored by weights. Frayed dust scurried about him. But a sudden anxiety hurtled through his limbs: he stood up, wiping the meandering blood from his nose and ear. Damn her and her illness and strangeness. And damn himself for hurting her again. His hands were crazy. From the window be noticed the pick-up gone. Christ! She couldn't do this. He was going to see her sitting with the car, faint in the darkness, parked half-way down the road. But he was out the door and he didn't. Patty had been fat and still; now she was skinny and what could she do? It was dark outside like a pit. He stumbled back inside. The clock ticked. He saw how things set a man up to fail, to twist on himself. Maybe now she was telling strangers everything. A black space opened up and began growing around him. He loved her. He poured himself a gin, but he dashed it to the floor, watched. He poured another and swallowed. It was illegal to leave like that.)

The room was very still. The sun came in, in orange rectangles. The sky glowed, part violet and part blue. She found a cup. There was only water to drink. She took a bath in the separated bathroom. Every sound was loud. She thought about how she was nothing to the world. She was so hungry; there was no food. Patricia lay down on the mattress and shut her eyes tightly.

In the morning, she wrote a letter to her mother:

Dear momma, Joe lied to you about my jaw. It was he who smashed it. I left home. I am looking for a job and soon enough will get one because it's very good for women these days. I live in a beautiful flowered room, momma. You'll be proud of me. I need $200.00 just to start me. Please can you lend it?

She wrote down the laundromat address Frank had given her, with a *P. S. It would be very dangerous if Joe knew where I was. Thank you, momma.*

Patricia searched through the cupboards and drawers. She found a fire escape ladder made of rope. It had rings that latched onto two hooks sticking out of the windowsill by the kitchenette. She didn't find anything else. She fished in her pants' pocket and lifted out the two teeth she had saved from her jaw smashing, then put them in the drawer with the rope. She was going to drive to Pierre. She stopped to ask Frank for directions. "Straight on route 34," he said. "Don't you let anyone talk to you funny and ruin that nice poetry you got inside, Pretty Eyes."

Patricia went to Goodwill and bought sheets, a pair of cotton pants, and shirts. She purchased a plate, glass, fork, knife and spoon, and a small bowl. A helper told her about a radio for $2.50 and gave her hangers. The tellers were very fast and easy at the bank. And, at the Motor Vehicles building, a lady with silvery glasses was pleasant. Because momma had given them money for the pick-up, Patricia's name was on the registration. The lady handed over shiny new plates.

Frank was happy to see her back. She paid him. "We got our money matters settled, didn't we?" Frank said. "I'm telling you straight; I wish there were more like you."

From her apartment window, Patricia looked out to the sunset and the grasses with golden insects jumping in them. The air smelled like honey. Her papers, all her words, were laid out over the kitchen table. She turned on the radio and listened to "Wheeler Dealer," and the weather coming ahead, and the world, how it made decisions. The military said armies and missiles were creeping in. An old actress died in bed. A baby had its eyes operated on for free because his mother wrote to the President. She heard the neighbors' dog bark. The wind whistled as if this was the strangest place on earth.

Then her neighbors wrote her a note:

On weekends don't turn the radio on so loud, please.

She had seen them. They saw her, and nodded their crunched-up fat faces and shut the door behind them, on her. Their dog was tied to a chain and when it barked awhile the husband went out and kicked it. Then it whimpered.

After a while, they wrote another note:

We don't know what kind of shoes you wear, but they stomp right over our heads. Could you please wear slippers?

She went for a walk. She stared into the low sun. A breeze seemed to run from it, to her, sweeping through her hair, rustling the grasses in a topaz light. She tried to speak to it all but did not know what to say. Those people had complaint in their hearts. Their words were ugly, wanting to hush her. They knew nothing. She was scared they would discover everything. She tried to write a poem and she had ached because another, new and dark face to words had hovered before her. Her answer wasn't so simple anymore. The breeze was fresh and kept blowing. She found wild irises tangled in the weeds; suddenly, she began clipping them with her fingernails. She gathered them up, but threw them down. They scattered, falling on their purple heads.

Frank came to visit her, in the morning, with an envelope. Her mother had written:

Are you all right? Love, momma, and enclosed a check.

Frank said, "I've missed you. You keep having your mail sent to the laundromat. I've got to go now, to pick up people's rents. It's a sad thing. Folks barely open their curtains to you. Don't you ever think it's lonely, Pretty Eyes?

She looked at him. She thought she wanted to say something

nice to him, very softly, but she couldn't think what. She decided to write Frank a poem. It needed to be happy. In the morning, on a sheet of blue paper, she brought it to him:

He got a blue baseball cap

And the walls are azure.

The whirr's from the machines,

Making everybody clean.

You say, "Two quarters and a dime."

Boy, you are feeling just fine.

Your shirt is white

Ready to fight

The light

Of the sun

When you run for fun

Don't forget your laundromat:

Maybe it's where you sat

A lot and thought

Eating a donut,

Being a poet.

"It's fantastic. It's about you and me," Frank said. He put his arm around her. But his hand made her scared to move. She thought his hand would twist on her, if she upset him. She had made the poem a provocation. A dry noise caught in her throat. "Oh, honey," Frank said. "Didn't anyone ever thank you?"

"Oh," she said.

His hand tightened on her like a wrench. She didn't know why she had never found the way things should be done so she wouldn't become prey.

"I'm going to frame it, honey," Frank said softly. "Nobody'll hurt it."

Frank visited her a week later. "I met your brother. Where's he gone to? Did you see him?" When Frank left, Patricia drove to Pierre. A locksmith returned with her and installed a steel rod lock on her apartment door.

When it was dark and late, she heard a car drive up, then a knock on her neighbors' door. There were murmurs, then their door clicked shut. Voices began speaking underneath her: Joe's voice. She tried to imagine what he had said so as to be allowed inside their house. He knew how to talk. A wind rattled her windows. The wife said, "Why yes, we guessed it. And today with a man hammering at her door. The landlord's been coming over, finding excuses to talk to her. We thought this wasn't regular. I'm sorry to hear this happened to you. A home's not a home any more. We thought the world'd gone crazy. You poor man. Well, we've only got a couple more weeks here, thank God."

Patricia's heart beat hard and jerky. She thought of Frank, how confused and hurt he was by people who ran.

Joe left. Patricia sat in her apartment for days and her food ran out. She could not sleep because of nightmares. Her sleeplessness made her dismayed every minute. She imagined escapes, but she saw Joe waiting for her. Police cars would surround her and the men would stare from their seats; they'd say: "an eye for an eye." She wouldn't be able to explain their misinterpretation to them. Empty fields stared at her; Joe's hands lifted. All she needed was her pick-up, but there was a one-way road out only. She thought this was a dream, how it all closed in on her so quickly.

Joe returned, beginning to help the neighbors unload boxes from their house for UPS. He looked strong and large and intent. The husband said, "If you're going to stay here, you want the mutt?"

Joe said, "Sure, a man's best friend."

The fat husband muttered, "Yeah."

Joe took the boxes away. Her neighbors remained like guards. Patricia's eyes were red, shrinking under her lids. She wanted Frank to come, but she'd have to cover her face with her hands if she saw him, and he wouldn't know what had happened. If she told him, he would think he hadn't known her at all. She didn't want him to think she had lied.

When Frank came and knocked on her door, she did not move. He left mail in her box. Patricia watched him walk away and get into his car, thin and bent up. She fetched her mail. Joe had never written to her before:

I found you, honey. I ask forgiveness for everything I did. And if you're scared you injured me, don't worry. It was a scratch. I want to start a new life with you. I was always meant for you. You been lost, honey. I will wait. I am going to be downstairs when these neighbors are moved. Why don't you start being softened up? Patty, this is a love note, honey. Joe.

Patricia's heart hurt. Momma wrote, too:

Now, Patty, Joe wrote to me about what they tried to do to you at the hospital. The way they were doctrinating you with ideas of women's lib which I tell you only women who have no heart and salt in their brains are going to tell you. They try to make women like me to be of no account when it strikes me as funny that they probably never had a husband to love them. Joe told me how you went wild and he wants you to get the right kind of help. And I want you to know that when you get home, then I'll come visit you and we'll have real good times together. Momma

P. S. And I am not sending you any more money, for what you've done is wrong.

Patricia cried and the wet letters wrinkled. There was one more to open:

Pretty Eyes, it said, *I got the poem framed. I miss you. The afternoons are very hot. We'll have brush fires soon. You take special care of that poetry I gave you. Come and do your laundry soon. Frank.*

Patricia thought about how many abandoned people you met who were lonely inside, like stray dogs. Then she remembered how she was being pursued. That was lonely, too. Patricia had tricked Frank; his heart had gotten played with just the way he said it always did. Joe had discovered her and now he would always hold her. She would become numb and fat. She tried hard to remember how poetry made you see new patterns; there was something in her that she had to look for. The fields were quiet. Joe came into her mind, sitting in front of the fireplace; a drop of sweat fell in his gin, he drank it. He never noticed how he ate himself. He watched the fire. She had been staring at the sunset. The sky was orange. It now told her clearly what to do.

Her neighbors were leaving. They wore new straw hats. "It's Florida," they said.

"Hell of a suntanning place," Joe said. "Don't mind me if I'm on your tail a short ways—I've got to get to Pierre for license plates now that I'll be installing myself in these parts."

The wife said, "We would like to buy you supper. You've been so nice to us and we wish you well. May we treat you?"

"I never turn down good company," Joe said. The cars left.

Patricia was startled. It was not a decision to be postponed. She began to move fast. She removed the sheets from her bed and stretched them on the floor. She hung the blanket over a window, then crumpled newspaper into wads and placed them in the cupboards, on the chairs, and the sofa. She knew about insurance, the money that could be made. The radio had talked about it one day. Nobody would be hurt. She took her two old teeth out and put them on the floor. She put her poetry in her pocket. The teeth would be here, later. The doors had to be locked from the inside. She hung the rope ladder out the window. There would be money for everybody. Frank's life would be easier. Patricia lit a match. It was like lighting a birthday cake: her eyes shimmered. Little flames licked up, while the red sunset came in like rubies. It seemed to her maybe there was more strangeness than not, to win the world with.

She climbed down the ladder; no one was about. The dog barked. She had newspapers under her arm and tore up some dry grass. She locked the main door, surprised it had been open. She stuffed the pile of dry things part-way under the door and put three matches to the edges. Flames blew out of the upstairs windows. Then she saw the back of Joe's car parked on the side of the house she had no windows to see it from. She stepped into the pick-up and began to drive. In the rearview mirror only dust appeared. Her heart would open. She would find poems for this, of beginnings.

(The light was wide and open around here, the fields like a great big doormat to heaven—so much so a man felt almost small. Joe was thinking maybe a man shouldn't ask for so much in this world, but a home and a woman in it ought to be his rights. He knew Patricia listened behind that house's curtains. She would hear him talk about license plates, would try to leave the house.

He had to surprise her. He stopped down the road, thanked the old couple, saying he'd forgotten some important papers in his suitcase, at their house. On the seat next to him, was a bouquet of purple violets curling up fast. He had the keys to the house and he was coming in now. He saw Patricia's soft, plump hands, in his mind, and her worried eyes like tired little stars. When she had left, his solitude was like a tunnel. He thought his heart was burning him; he drank but he couldn't get cool enough. The drink grabbed him and pulled him to the God awful darkness. When he drove back, he didn't find Patricia at the window but the pick-up was there. Joe unlocked the front door, holding the violets like a beacon leading him up the steps. Then he stood before the two doors, and decided to slip into the bathroom first. He shut the door, and tried to think of how to talk to her, to stop her from writing those damned deaf-and-dumb notes. He filled the sink with water for the flowers. Then began to wash himself up, dipping her yellow washrag into the water. He wanted to touch Patricia. He heard a rustling. There was a peculiar smell. Joe saw a piece of light lick up from under the bathroom door, but suddenly he was numb. One night, he had fallen into a drunken stupor. Startled by a noise, he had awoken staring into a huge fire. He had screamed. But it was just the hot fireplace, with calm, prancing flames. But they had followed him in his mind; they were a roar.)

10

The mob piled in. Heat. Sweat. Noise. Smoke.

The FIGHT! Stripped to the waist they clashed; local lads locked in combat!

Mallet spat blood, trod back, ducked, and blasted Gunter's neck. THUD! CRUNCH! SMACK!

Mallet hit the deck! SPLAT!

Mallet snored! ZZZZ! DING! Saved by the bell!

A wet rag slapped his map. 'Come on kid!' barked his boss. 'We need that cash for meat and that! Do 'im!'

Mallet launched a brutal attack!

Gunter caught a savage clout. THWACK! And dropped!

'...Seven...Eight...Nine...TEN!' OUT!

And that was that!

The End

From *BRUTE!* by Malcolm Bennett and Aidan Hughes. Copyright ©1988 by Malcolm Bennett and Aidan Hughes. Reprinted by permission of the authors.

11

Ah dear God, are they starting again? Is this them with their voices crackling at me from the light bulb again? And me thinking I wouldn't go through another night of it. I look at my fingers — they seem so far away from me, at first I think I see a crab of some type lying there on the open page, a yellow crab with horny pincers, a creature unrelated to me. I follow it up my arm to my shoulder, I need to do this to confirm that the thing is a part of me, or at any rate connected to this composite, this loosely assembled and unraveling weave of gristle, husk and bone. For I am almost empty now, the foul taste in my mouth attests to this, and of course the smell of gas, and I wonder (such are my thoughts at night) what they will find when they cut me open after death (if I'm not dead already)? An anatomical monstrosity, surely: my small intestine is wrapped tightly around the lower part of my spine and ascends in a taut snug spiral, thickening grossly into the colon about half-way up, which twists around my upper spine like a boa constrictor, the rectum passing through my skull and the anus issuing from the top of my head where an opening has been created between the bones joining the top of my skull, which I constantly finger in wondering horror, a sort of mature excretory fontanelle (my hair would be matted and stinking but for the blessed rain that daily cleanses me). Since this occurred (late one night earlier in the week) I have tried not to eat, for the movement of matter through the intestines has become painfully vivid to me, a series of jerky spasms as though a worm of some kind were crawling round my backbone. Other organs have been compressed against my skeleton so as to create a void or emptiness in the trunk of my body, and I haven't yet learned why this is occurring. One of my lungs has disappeared; there is a worm in the other but fortunately smoking remains possible. A single thin pipe takes water from my stomach (squashed flat and ridged against my rib cage) and this pipe alone drops through the void and connects to the thing between my legs that hardly resembles a formed male organ at all anymore. There is material rotting slowly inside me, the composting remains of organs I no longer need, and it is because the odors given off by this process have begun to seep through the pores of my skin (my skin! my husk, my shell, my *rind*!) that I have now wrapped my torso and all my limbs in newspaper and corrugated cardboard held in place with string, sticky tape, rubber bands, whatever I have been able to steal around the house. All this, all this I can live with; what preys upon my mind now is the thought that my body is being *prepared* for something, that I am being evacuated internally so as to *make room for something else*: and even as I write these words, even as I draw a wavering line beneath them, a loud cackle suddenly comes from the light bulb, and from the attic a volley of stamping that shakes the walls and sets the light bulb swinging on its cord, and I sit here terrified, clutching the table with both hands as the swinging bulb throws the room into wildly shifting blocks of light and shadow.

It subsides to a flicker and a crackle and I stand up from the table, I must leave the room if only for five minutes. I shuffle to the door and there's an ominous howl from above as I lay hands on the knob and turn it, but their wrath I can endure for a short time at least. Down the darkened landing to the lavatory, where I stand over the toilet and with trembling fingers unbutton my trousers. A small pipelike apparatus, something from a plumber's toolbox, protrudes and begins urinating tiny black spiders into the bowl, where they curl up into points and float on the water. I appear to be infested; I appear to be playing host to a colony of spiders; I appear to be an *egg-bag*.

Back in my room I stand at the table leaning on my hands and gaze out at the leafless trees in the park below. Illuminated dimly by the glow of the street lamp, their fingery boughs form a pale tracery against the darkness. The night sky is cloudy, there is no moon. Nothing is moving out there. I sink with a rustle of news-print and cardboard into my chair and pick up my pencil. I'd thought I wouldn't go through another night of it; in this as in all else I am wrong, I delude myself with the idea that I am *free*, have *control*, can *act*. It is not so. I am their creature.

12

I am a fly called Gilbert and I live by a pond, a stagnant pond in a bird sanctuary. The surface of the pond is covered by a carpet of tiny bright green organic discs. The reeds and the rushes still thrust up from the muddy bed below, and as the breeze plays over the water the leafy tendrils of a weeping willow on the bank stir gently. Climb the bank and you will find, set back in the trees, a tumbledown shed. This is where the E(ROT)IC POTATO is.

One day I flew up the bank where the shadows hang and the ivy claws at the gray stones edging flatly out of the irradiated earth. Forms of other insects flashed by me. I settled upon a branch and turned my compound eyes toward the shed which housed the E(ROT)IC POTATO. It lay beneath the trees, and though its windows were smashed and boarded up with cardboard, its roof was whole. The white paint was peeling off the boards, and the door was held closed by a rusty nail. One hinge hung loose. The sharp tap of a bird's beak rattled suddenly through the air. A butterfly emerged from between the cardboard and the shattered windowpane. A rusting tool, half in sunlight and half in shadow, was leaned against the wall beside the shaky door. I did not go further. I knew I would be turned back. I was not yet ready to enter the presence of the E(ROT)IC POTATO. The emergent butterfly drifted by me in the dappled woodland sunlight, and I returned to the pond.

On the way I found a fairly large crowd of insects gathered round a poisoned water rat, and the air was abuzz with the vibrations of fine wings and the chatter of excited voices. The creature lay on the bank shivering, for its pelt had lost the sleek oily texture that insulates the mammal within. After a few feeble attempts to haul its body up the bank it collapsed limply and lay panting, near death, in the mud. A yellow fluid seeped thickly from its ears and eyes, and a greenish discoloration spread across its soft underbelly. As the breathing grew heavier, the mouth opened and sucked air and we saw that its teeth had crumbled to impotent stumps. A rat without teeth was doomed, in our world.

Several flies and some ants had already mounted the body and were sampling tissue. They quickly discovered that the irradiation was mild, and once again we were confronted by proof of our biological superiority: that rat couldn't breathe our air and live. A warm pulse ran through the crowd, and then we set to.

There was more than enough for all, but naturally we wanted to lay open the belly first and get at the inner organs. The biters and chewers were quickly ushered to the front, and went to work. The rest of us buzzed about, making inroads where we could. I was set to breaking down blockage in the left ear, to clear a passage to the brain.

Sometime later word spread that the ants had got through, and we buzzed down to have a look. Ariadne the dragonfly had been flitting about the head for a while, and flew close to me on the short hop to the opened belly. I was thrilled by her proximity, and though our eyes did not meet I knew she was aware of me.

There was a buzzy crunch on the belly of the water rat, and in all the confusion of eager mandibles and flashing wings my body drew very close to Ariadne's. I felt a tremor run through her as my proboscis glanced against her articulated thorax, and then something rather wonderful happened. Ariadne fluttered aloft and, hovering close, delicately displayed the milkwhite tip of her ovipositor to me. I was flooded by an irresistible genetic impulse to penetrate and fertilize her, but the trembling organ was withdrawn and the flashing blue-green dragonfly fluttered away.

Then, before my reeling senses could recover, they were again bombarded, this time by a meaty waft of warm fresh mammalian intestine. At that point I lost control completely and plunged into the innards of the rat's body with my fellows and fed.

The meal continued as the sun moved across an intensely brown sky. In the late afternoon, when the pond lay in shadow and nothing stirred the reeds, and the dripping tendrils of the weeping willow ululated imperceptibly and the tranquility was broken only by the endless declamations of the throstle-throated birds, and the countless tiny bright green organic discs had silently meshed to form an unbroken slimy weave over the poisoned water, the crab arrived.

"My turn, I think," he murmured as he eased his great plated frame sideways up the bank. There was a din of protest at this, but the crustacean could not have cared less for the shrill outrage of a fly. He thrust a massive claw into the cadaver; and then, in full view of the assembled insects, he scooped out and consumed a dripping, glistening mountain of our eggs! The uproar intensified, but with utter indifference the hoary old scavenger shuffled his cantankerous and exoskeletal self entirely inside the rat's body, and within a few moments a steady, muffled grumble, basso profundo, was all that could be heard. He emerged, some time later, eructating, and made his way sideways back to the pond.

That night Ariadne admitted me to the E(ROT)IC POTATO. In a darkness strangely alive we flew from the body of the dead rat up the bank and through the trees to the shed. A full moon, tinted with toxins to the color of a rotting orange, bathed our rickety little temple in the febrile glow of postapocalyptic romance. Ariadne's articulated rear segment trailed through the moonbeams and I flew steadily in her wake, inhaling drunkenly the subtle wisplets of insect love juice she was secreting. She landed with grace upon the edge of the windowframe and I came down beside her a moment later, swooning foolishly, barely conscious.

There were wasps everywhere. They swarmed about the shattered windowframe and squeezed themselves between the shards and the cardboard in the moonlight. Ariadne, her long smooth gauzy wings folded perpendicular above herself, twitched her slender tail sharply as one of these guardians approached us. I knew enough to let her do the talking.

"Good evening," said the wasp smoothly.

Ariadne, rubbing her gossamer wings one against the other and filling the air with a silky rustle that excited me beyond words, graced the handsome big stinger with a dazzling multi-faceted glance.

"Ariadne," said the wasp, with pleasure. "And — a small fly?" I blew out my bulbous thorax, somewhat pricked by his tone.

"Roger, isn't it?" murmured Ariadne, and as the wasp inclined his head with slight irony, she went on briskly, "Yes, I shall be taking him in with me."

Then she rose into the air and hovered there, flicking her tail. "No problem, is there, Roger?" she breathed, glancing down at the wasp.

"None at all," he said, and with a small smile playing about his segmented lower mouthpart, he ushered her through the broken windowpane, I prepared to follow.

"Out late, little fly," remarked the wasp. "Fancied a bit of dragonfly, did we?"

The way he pronounced the word *dragonfly* left me in no doubt as to his meaning. It was a scurrilous imputation—so I buzzed him.

"Brat!" hissed the enraged yellowjacket, his sting-charged rear end whipping upward like a scorpion's. I zipped at high speed through the laser-thin gap between the shards and the call-board and swept abuzzing into the temple of the E(ROT)IC POTATO.

And was immediately stopped short in my trajectory by the sheer majesty of the spectacle that lay before me. Ariadne hovered near a moonlit rafter and, wordlessly stupefied, thrilled beyond language, I joined her. Together we gazed down from the high regions of its cathedral upon the splendor of the E(ROT)IC POTATO.

It was a dead man lying on his back under a table, with one hand on his breast and the other on a book on the floor. His chest had caved in and the hand itself had flopped limply into the cavity where once had been the heart. The heart itself, of course, was long since devoured.

And the man's eyes and ears and mouth and belly were alive with insects! And the space between his body and the table was filled with flying insects! And their sounds were amplified by the gabled roof and filled the gloomy chamber like the very drone of Eternity itself! And that vast booming buzzing harmony was a sonic articulation of the Triumph of the Insect Will!

"Come, Gilbert," whispered Ariadne, and I followed her through the shafts of orange moonlight and descended with reverence deep into the bowels of the E(ROT)IC POTATO. There, in the darkness, I observed once again the milkwhite miracle of her ovipositor; but this time the organ was not withdrawn.

And then every dawning genetic tremor I had ever felt was finally fulfilled, not once, not twice, but a thousand times! A million times! A thousand million times! I quivered to the very quick of my being; I surrendered, fragmented, melted in the molten intolerable pleasure of it and dissolved to pure nonbeing, wrapped in shattering slithering Ariadne and sinking deeper and ever-deeper into the glow and pulse of the degenerating intestine of the E(ROT)IC POTATO.

Later, still intoxicated, I lurched out, creamed and filmed with the eggy juices of insect love, and crawled away to lick my wings. The dull buzz of Eternity roared warmly through my drained and sated body, and I knew I was changed forever. As the moon sank to the horizon and the first brown rays of a new day probed the eastern sky, I knew I had finally become a fly.

13

Privileged
Touches
intense
converse
undertow

between
this
love
and
its
body
obstacle

between
is
and
is
not
off
and
on

You do not know.
Will it happen or
when will it end?
Afraid to touch a hot
iron.
Don't anticipate or
direct.
Aimed a touch too low
and missed.
Wait watch, observe
and ride. Stimulate,
massaging outward
with circular
movements, starting
at the center between
and moving outward
and upward, around
the inward and
downward to the
starting point.
Touched by the
loyalty of his
friends.

Nancy Davidson

	Press and turn
	between your index
Very	finger and thumb,
clear	breathing deeply.
touches	Follow the movements
soft	that feel right for
light	you.
gaseous	Touched by fever.
liquid	You can choose to do
hairless	this with two hands
parts	or one hand. Don't
soles	get to the point of
fingertips	no return.
clitoris	Never touches alcohol
penis	in any form.
nipples	It is enough to
palm	generate warmth, a
tongue	tingling sensation.
over	If you have a
the	pleasant feeling,
blue	continue.
bed	Your things haven't
open	been touched while
to	you were away.
the	If necessary
lip	stimulate once again.
and	Slowly excite each
litter	other, taking turns
of	giving and receiving.
desire	One can massage while
	the other gently
	strokes.
memory	Don't touch anything
nerve	until the police
skin	come.
	Then exchange roles.

Clear
touches
ongoing
narrative
vary
time
spent
exploring
skin
surface
work
us

Muffled
touches
no
relationship
abrasion
brushing
fumbling
tattoo
girl's
nape
noli
me
tangere
between
fact
and
truth

two
scripts

When you feel open to
further exploration,
change positions. It
is important to have
the front part in
close contact.
Strictly his affair,
I wouldn't touch it
for anything.

Keep movement to a
minimum.
Their farm touches
the river.
The more focused on
your own sensations,
the more you will
perceive the rhythms
that you share.
If you feel you are
coming close through
these subtleties,
make sure you don't.
Fruit touched by
On the other hand, if
at any time you feel
you are slipping,
return until you have
restored a sense of
mutual arousal.

Touches
of
ambient
conversation
subject
guests
scrap
heat
war
impossible
to
fragment
to
divide
sharp
angular
places
curve
fullness
between
said
and
done

crack
crevice
opening
cut
streak
groove
wrinkle
trace
scar
notch

The lines though
touched faintly are
drawn right.
Touch loosely so that
a little outside air
is incorporated into
the exchange.
Rest and relax inside
each other for ten to
fifteen minutes.
Be in a good mood
before you begin.
Remain relaxed and
light about it.
They sat with their
heads nearly
touching.
You may get impatient
or be discouraged
because you are not
feeling much.
Have a firm touch.
You may feel a little
clumsy, but with
practice it will get
easier.
Review in front of
each other.
A touch of unreality
about the whole
affair.
Remember to have fun!
If things don't flow
easily, don't push.

change
places
often
as
you
like

14

"The Théâtre des Vampires was by invitation only, and the next night the doorman inspected my card for a moment while the rain fell softly all around us: on the man and woman stopped at the shut-up box office; on the crinkling posters of penny-dreadful vampires with their outstretched arms and cloaks resembling bat wings ready to close on the naked shoulders of a mortal victim; on the couple that pressed past us into the packed lobby, where I could easily perceive that the crowd was all human, no vampires among them, not even this boy who admitted us finally into the press of conversation and damp wool and ladies' gloved fingers fumbling with felt-brimmed hats and wet curls. I pressed for the shadows in a feverish excitement. We had fed earlier only so that in the bustling street of this theater our skin would not be too white, our eyes too unclouded. And that taste of blood which I had not enjoyed had left me all the more uneasy; but I had no time for it. This was no night for killing. This was to be a night of revelations, no matter how it ended. I was certain.

"Yet here we stood with this all too human crowd, the doors opening now on the auditorium, and a young boy pushing towards us, beckoning, pointing above the shoulders of the crowd to the stairs. Ours was a box, one of the best in the house, and if the blood had not dimmed my skin completely nor made Claudia into a human child as she rode in my arms, this usher did not seem at all to notice it nor to care. In fact, he smiled all too readily as he drew back the curtain for us on two chairs before the brass rail.

"'Would you put it past them to have human slaves?' Claudia whispered.

"'But Lestat never trusted human slaves,' I answered. I watched the seats fill, watched the marvelously flowered hats navigating below me through the rows of silk chairs. White shoulders gleamed in the deep curve of the balcony spreading out from us; diamonds glittered in the gas light. 'Remember, be sly for once,' came Claudia's whisper from beneath her bowed blond head. 'You're too much of a gentleman.'

"The lights were going out, first in the balcony, and then along the walls of the main floor. A knot of musicians had gathered in the pit below the stage, and at the foot of the long, green velvet curtain the gas flickered, then brightened, and the audience receded as if enveloped by a gray cloud through which only diamonds sparkled, on wrists, on throats, on fingers. And a hush descended like that gray cloud until all the sound was collected in one echoing persistent cough. Then silence. And the slow, rhythmical beating of a tambourine. Added to that was the thin melody of a wooden flute, which seemed to pick up the sharp metallic tink of the bells of the tambourine, winding them into a haunting melody that was medieval in sound. Then the strumming of strings that emphasized the tambourine. And the flute rose, in that melody singing of something melancholy, sad. It had a charm to it, this music, and the whole audience seemed stilled and united by it, as if the music of that flute were a luminous ribbon unfurling slowly in the dark. Not even the rising curtain broke the silence with the slightest sound. The lights brightened, and it seemed the stage was not the stage but a thickly wooded place, the light glittering on the roughened tree trunks and the thick clusters of leaves beneath the arch of darkness above; and through the trees could be seen what appeared to be the low, stone bank of a river and above that, beyond that, the glittering waters of the river itself, this whole three-dimensional world produced in painting upon a fine silk scrim that shivered only slightly in a faint draft.

"A sprinkling of applause greeted the illusion, gathering adherents from all parts of the auditorium until it reached its short crescendo and died away. A dark, draped figure was moving on the stage from tree trunk to tree trunk, so fast that as he stepped into the lights he seemed to appear magically in the center, one arm flashing out from his cloak to show a silver scythe and the other to hold a mask on a slender stick before the invisible face, a mask which showed the gleaming countenance of Death, a painted skull.

"There were gasps from the crowd. It was Death standing before the audience, the scythe poised, Death at the edge of a dark wood. And something in me was responding now as the audience responded, not in fear, but in some human way, to the magic of that fragile painted set, the mystery of the lighted world there, the world in which this figure moved in his billowing black cloak, back and forth before the audience with the grace of a great panther, drawing forth, as it were, those gasps, those sighs, those reverent murmurs.

"And now, behind this figure, whose very gestures seemed to have a captivating power like the rhythm of the music to which it moved, came other figures from the wings. First an old woman, very stooped and bent, her gray hair like moss, her arm hanging down with the weight of a great basket of flowers. Her shuttling steps scraped on the stage, and her head bobbed with the rhythm of the music and the darting steps of the Grim Reaper. And then she started back as she laid eyes on him and, slowly setting down her basket, made her hands into the attitude of prayer. She was tired; her head leaned now on her hands as if in sleep, and she reached out for him, supplicating. But as he came towards her, he bent to look directly into her face, which was all shadows to us beneath her hair, and started back then, waving his hand as if to freshen the air. Laughter erupted uncertainly from the audience. But as the old woman rose and took after Death, the laughter took over.

"The music broke into a jig with their running, as round and round the stage the old woman pursued Death, until he finally flattened himself into the dark of a tree trunk, bowing his masked face under his wing like a bird. And the old woman, lost, defeated, gathered up her basket as the music softened and slowed to her pace, and made her way off the stage. I did not like it. I did not like the laughter. I could see the other figures moving in now, the music orchestrating their gestures, cripples on crutches and beggars with rags the color of ash, all reaching out for Death, who whirled, escaping this one with a sudden arching of the back, fleeing from that one with an effeminate gesture of disgust, waving them all away finally in a foppish display of weariness and boredom.

"It was then I realized that the languid, white hand that made these comic arcs was not painted white. It was a vampire hand which wrung laughter from the crowd. A vampire hand lifted now to the grinning skull, as the stage was finally clear, as if stifling a yawn. And then this vampire, still holding the mask before his face, adopted marvelously the attitude of resting his weight against a painted silken tree, as if he were falling gently to sleep. The music twittered like birds, rippled like the flowing of the water; and the spotlight, which encircled him in a yellow pool, grew dim, all but fading away as he slept.

"And another spot pierced the scrim, seeming to melt it altogether, to reveal a young woman standing alone far upstage. She was majestically tall and all but enshrined by a voluminous mane of golden blond hair. I could feel the awe of the audience as she seemed to flounder in the spotlight, the dark forest rising on the perimeter, so that she seemed to be lost in the trees. And she was lost; and not a vampire. The soil on her mean blouse and skirt was not stage paint, and nothing had touched her perfect face, which gazed into the light now, as beautiful and finely chiseled as the face of a marble Virgin, that hair her haloed veil. She could not see in the light, though all could see her. And the moan which escaped her lips as she floundered seemed to echo over the thin, romantic singing of the flute, which was a tribute to that beauty. The figure of Death woke with a start in his pale spotlight and turned to see her as the audience had seen her, and to throw up his free hand in tribute, in awe.

"The twitter of laughter died before it became real. She was too beautiful, her gray eyes too distressed. The performance too perfect. And then the skull mask was thrown suddenly into the wings and Death showed a beaming white face to the audience, his hurried hands stroking his handsome black hair, straightening a waistcoat, brushing imaginary dust from his lapels. Death in love. And clapping rose for the luminous countenance, the gleaming cheekbones, the winking black eye, as if it were all masterful illusion when in fact it was merely and certainly the face of a vampire, the vampire who had accosted me in the Latin Quarter, that leering, grinning vampire, harshly illuminated by the yellow spot.

"My hand reached for Claudia's in the dark and pressed it tightly. But she sat still, as if enrapt. The forest of the stage, through which that helpless mortal girl stared blindly towards the laughter, divided in two phantom halves, moving away from the center, freeing the vampire to close in on her.

"And she who had been advancing towards the footlights, saw him suddenly and came to a halt, making a moan like a child. Indeed, she was very like a child, though clearly a full-grown woman. Only a slight wrinkling of the tender flesh around her eyes betrayed her age. Her breasts though small were beautifully shaped beneath her blouse, and her hips though narrow gave her long, dusty skirt a sharp, sensual angularity. As she moved back from the vampire, I saw the tears standing in her eyes like glass in the flicker of the lights, and I felt my spirit contract in fear for her, and in longing. Her beauty was heartbreaking.

"Behind her, a number of painted skulls suddenly moved against the blackness, the figures that carried the masks invisible in their black clothes, except for free white hands that clasped the edge of a cape, the folds of a skirt. Vampire women were there, moving in with the men towards the victim, and now they all, one by one, thrust the masks away so they fell in an artful pile, the sticks like bones, the skulls grinning into the darkness above. And there they stood, seven vampires, the women vampires three in number, their molded white breasts shining over the tight black bodices of their gowns, their hard luminescent faces staring with dark eyes beneath curls of black hair. Starkly beautiful, as they seemed to float close around that florid human figure, yet pale and cold compared to that sparkling golden hair, that petal-pink skin. I could hear the breath of the audience, the halting, the soft sighs. It was a spectacle, that circle of white faces pressing closer and closer, and that leading figure, that Gentleman Death, turning to the audience now with his hands crossed over his heart, his head bent in longing to elicit their sympathy: was she not irresistible! A murmur of accenting laughter, of sighs.

"But it was she who broke the magic silence.

"'I don't want to die...' she whispered. Her voice was like a bell.

"'We *are* death,' he answered her; and from around her came the whisper, 'Death.' She turned, tossing her hair so it became a veritable shower of gold, a rich and living thing over the dust of her poor clothing. 'Help me!' she cried out softly, as if afraid even to raise her voice. 'Someone...' she said to the crowd she knew must be there. A soft laughter came from Claudia. The girl on stage only vaguely understood where she was, what was happening, but knew infinitely more than this house of people that gaped at her.

"'I don't want to die! I don't want to!' Her delicate voice broke, her eyes fixed on the tall, malevolent leader vampire, that demon trickster who now stepped out of the circle of the others towards her.

"'We all die,' he answered her. 'The one thing you share with every mortal is death.' His hand took in the orchestra, the distant faces of the balcony, the boxes.

"'No,' she protested in disbelief. 'I have so many years, so many...' Her voice was light, lilting in her pain. It made her irresistible, just as did the movement of her naked throat and the hand that fluttered there.

"'Years!' said the master vampire. 'How do you know you have so many years? Death is no respecter of age! There could be a sickness in your body now, already devouring you from within. Or, outside, a man might be waiting to kill simply for your yellow hair!' And his fingers reached for it, the sound of his deep, preternatural voice sonorous. 'Need I tell what fate may have in store for you?'

"'I don't care...I'm not afraid,' she protested, her clarion voice so fragile after him. 'I would take my chance....'

"'And if you do take that chance and live, live for years, what would be your heritage? The humpbacked, toothless visage of old age?' And now he lifted her hair behind her back, exposing her pale throat. And slowly he drew the string from the loose gathers of her blouse. The cheap fabric opened, the sleeves slipping off her narrow, pink shoulders; and she clasped it, only to have him take her wrists and thrust them sharply away. The audience seemed to sigh in a body, the women behind their opera glasses, the men leaning forward in their chairs. I could see the cloth falling, see the pale, flawless skin pulsing with her heart and the tiny nipples letting the cloth slip precariously, the vampire holding her right wrist tightly at her side, the tears coursing down her blushing cheeks, her teeth biting into the flesh of her lip. 'Just as sure as this flesh is pink, it will turn gray, wrinkled with age,' he said.

"'Let me live, please,' she begged, her face turning away from him. 'I don't care...I don't care.'

"'Then, why should you care if you die now? If these things don't frighten you...these horrors?'

"She shook her head, baffled, outsmarted, helpless. I felt the anger in my veins, as sure as the passion. With a bowed head she bore the whole responsibility for defending life, and it was unfair, monstrously unfair that she should have to pit logic against his for what was obvious and sacred and so beautifully embodied in her. But he made her speechless, made her overwhelming instinct seem petty, confused. I could feel her dying inside, weakening, and I hated him.

"The blouse slipped to her waist. A murmur moved through the titillated crowd as her small, round breasts stood exposed. She struggled to free her wrist, but he held it fast.

"'And suppose we were to let you go...suppose the Grim Reaper had a heart that could resist your beauty...to whom would he turn his passion? Someone must die in your place. Would you pick the person for us? The person to stand here and suffer as you suffer now?' He gestured to the audience. Her confusion was terrible. 'Have you a sister...a mother...a child?'

"'No,' she gasped. 'No . . .' shaking the mane of hair.

"'Surely someone could take your place, a friend? Choose!'

"'I can't. I wouldn't. . . .' She writhed in his tight grasp. The vampires around her looked on, still, their faces evincing no emotion, as if the preternatural flesh were masks. 'Can't you do it?' he taunted her. And I knew, if she said she could, how he would only condemn her, say she was as evil as he for marking someone for death, say that she deserved her fate.

"'Death waits for you everywhere,' he sighed now as if he were suddenly frustrated. The audience could not perceive it, I could. I could see the muscles of his smooth face tightening. He was trying to keep her gray eyes on his eyes, but she looked desperately, hopefully away from him. On the warm, rising air I could smell the dust and perfume of her skin, hear the soft beating of her heart. 'Unconscious death . . . the fate of all mortals.' He bent closer to her, musing, infatuated with her, struggling. 'Hmmm. . . . but we are *conscious* death! That would make you a bride. Do you know what it means to be loved by Death?' He all but kissed her face, the brilliant stain of her tears. 'Do you know what it means to have Death know your name?'

"She looked at him, overcome with fear. And then her eyes seemed to mist over, her lips to go slack. She was staring past him at the figure of another vampire who had emerged slowly from the shadows. For a long time he had stood on the periphery of the gathering, his hands clasped, his large, dark eyes very still. His attitude was not the attitude of hunger. He did not appear rapt. But she was looking into his eyes now, and her pain bathed her in a beauteous light, a light which made her irresistibly alluring. It was this that held the jaded audience, this terrible pain. I could feel her skin, feel the small, pointed breasts, feel my arms caressing her. I shut my eyes against it and saw her starkly against that private darkness. It was what they felt all around her, this community of vampires. She had no chance.

"And, looking up again, I saw her shimmering in the smoky light of the footlamps, saw her tears like gold as soft from that other vampire who stood at a distance came the words . . . 'No pain.'

"I could see the trickster stiffen, but no one else would see it. They would see only the girl's smooth, childlike face, those parted lips, slack with innocent wonder as she gazed at that distant vampire, hear her soft voice repeat after him, 'No pain?'

"'Your beauty is a gift to us.' His rich voice effortlessly filled the house, seemed to fix and subdue the mounting wave of excitement. And slightly, almost imperceptibly, his hand moved. The trickster was receding, becoming one of those patient, white faces, whose hunger and equanimity were strangely one. And slowly, gracefully, the other moved towards her. She was languid, her nakedness forgotten, those lids fluttering, a sigh escaping her moist lips. 'No pain,' she accented. I could hardly bear it, the sight of her yearning towards him, seeing her dying now, under this vampire's power. I wanted to cry out to her, to break her swoon. And I wanted her. Wanted her, as he was moving in on her, his hand out now for the drawstring of her skirt as she inclined towards him, her head back, the black cloth slipping over her hips, over the golden gleam of the hair between her legs — a child's down, that delicate curl — the skirt dropping to her feet. And this vampire opened his arms, his back to the flickering footlights, his auburn hair seeming to tremble as the gold of her hair fell around his black coat. 'No pain...no pain...' he was whispering to her, and she was giving herself over.

"And now, turning her slowly to the side so that they could all see her serene face, he was lifting her, her back arching as her naked breasts touched his buttons, her pale arms enfolded his neck. She stiffened, cried out as he sank his teeth, and her face was still as the dark theater reverberated with shared passion. His white hand shone on her florid buttocks, her hair dusting it, stroking it. He lifted her off the boards as he drank, her throat gleaming against his white cheek. I felt weak, dazed, hunger rising in me, knotting my heart, my veins. I felt my hand gripping the brass bar of the box, tighter, until I could feel the metal creaking in its joints. And that soft, wrenching sound which none of those mortals might hear seemed somehow to hook me to the solid place where I was.

"I bowed my head; I wanted to shut my eyes. The air seemed

fragrant with her salted skin, and close and hot and sweet. Around her the other vampires drew in, the white hand that held her tight quivered, and the auburn-haired vampire let her go, turning her, displaying her, her head fallen back as he gave her over, one of those starkly beautiful vampire women rising behind her, cradling her, stroking her as she bent to drink. They were all about her now, as she was passed from one to another and to another, before the enthralled crowd, her head thrown forward over the shoulder of a vampire man, the nape of her neck as enticing as the small buttocks or the flawless skin of her long thighs, the tender creases behind her limply bent knees.

"I was sitting back in the chair, my mouth full of the taste of her, my veins in torment. And in the corner of my eyes was that auburn-haired vampire who had conquered her, standing apart as he had been before, his dark eyes seeming to pick me from the darkness, seeming to fix on me over the currents of warm air.

"One by one the vampires were withdrawing. The painted forest came back, sliding soundlessly into place. Until the mortal girl, frail and very white, lay naked in that mysterious wood, nestled in the silk of a black bier as if on the floor of the forest itself; and the music had begun again, eerie and alarming, growing louder as the lights grew dimmer. All the vampires were gone, except for the trickster, who had gathered his scythe from the shadows and also his hand-held mask. And he crouched near the sleeping girl as the lights slowly faded, and the music alone had power and force in the enclosing dark. And then that died also.

"For a moment, the entire crowd was utterly still.

"Then applause began here and there and suddenly united everyone around us. The lights rose in the sconces on the walls and heads turned to one another, conversation erupting all round. A woman rising in the middle of a row to pull her fox fur sharply from the chair, though no one had yet made way for her; someone else pushing out quickly to the carpeted aisle; and the whole body was on its feet as if driven to the exits.

"But then the hum became the comfortable, jaded hum of the sophisticated and perfumed crowd that had filled the lobby and the vault of the theater before. The spell was broken. The doors were flung open on the fragrant rain, the clop of horses' hooves, and voices calling for taxis. Down in the sea of slightly askew chairs, a white glove gleamed on a green silk cushion.

"I sat watching, listening, one hand shielding my lowered face from anyone and no one, my elbow resting on the rail, the passion in me subsiding, the taste of the girl on my lips. It was as though on the smell of the rain came her perfume still, and in the empty theater I could hear the throb of her beating heart. I sucked in my breath, tasted the rain, and glimpsed Claudia sitting infinitely still, her gloved hands in her lap.

"There was a bitter taste in my mouth, and confusion. And then I saw a lone usher moving on the aisle below, righting the chairs, reaching for the scattered programs that littered the carpet. I was aware that this ache in me, this confusion, this blinding passion which only let me go with a stubborn slowness would be obliterated if I were to drop down to one of those curtained archways beside him and draw him up fast in the darkness and take him as that girl was taken. I wanted to do it, and I wanted nothing. Claudia said near my bowed ear, 'Patience, Louis. Patience.'

"I opened my eyes. Someone was near, on the periphery of my vision; someone who had outsmarted my hearing, my keen anticipation, which penetrated like a sharp antenna even this distraction, or so I thought. But there he was, soundless, beyond the curtained entrance of the box, that vampire with the auburn hair, that detached one, standing on the carpeted stairway looking at us. I knew him now to be, as I'd suspected, the vampire who had given me the card admitting us to the theater. Armand.

"He would have startled me, except for his stillness, the remote dreamy quality of his expression. It seemed he'd been standing against that wall for the longest time, and betrayed no sign of change as we looked at him, then came towards him. Had he not so completely absorbed me, I would have been relieved he was not the tall, black-haired one; but I didn't think of this. Now his eyes moved languidly over Claudia with no tribute whatsoever to the human habit of disguising the stare. I placed my hand on Claudia's shoulder. 'We've been searching for you a very long time,' I said to him, my heart growing calmer, as if his calm were drawing off my trepidation, my care, like the sea drawing something into itself from the land. I cannot exaggerate this quality in him. Yet I can't describe it and couldn't then; and the fact that my mind sought to describe it even to myself unsettled me. He gave me the very feeling that he knew what I was doing, and his still posture and his deep, brown eyes seemed to say there was no use in what I was thinking, or particularly the words I was struggling to form now. Claudia said nothing.

"He moved away from the wall and began to walk down the stairs, while at the same time he made a gesture that welcomed us and bade us follow; but all this was fluid and fast. My gestures were the caricature of human gestures compared to his. He opened a door in the lower wall and admitted us to the rooms below the theater, his feet only brushing the stone stairway as we descended, his back to us with complete trust."

15

If I could snag your butt once, snatch you right down as you slither by I'd find out what makes you so hot. I'd cling firmly to the scruff of your feeble neck and snake my way down to sniff that magic butthole of yours. Himmler maybe found the center of the earth or the gateway to hell but I'd tinker with the brink of pure, holy emptiness. You'd be mine then rather than me inextricably yours (fuck you for that).

You've connivingly infected my dreams with the tumbles and splashes of discarded bodies off exotic cliffs, the skidding of heavy boots on slippery stones, the sound of slow-paced hoof-steps approaching. Seducing whistles and whispers echoed through the distant caverns of Death, the slapping, the muffled moans, the snapping and rips of muscle and bones: all this I dream and all this seems good. I know though, despite what you've said, that the dead are obviously much more clumsy and ignorant than you've made them out to be.

The dead have the willingness but, also, the ineptness of a toddler attempting its first solo toilet shit. They are like this: They see what they speak. They hear the sound of other's hearing. They feel without being able to discern what they've felt. They can walk, but never in a straight line. They can taste something at arm's length. They can disappear but they can't smell or even tie their own shoes. They moan; no consonants though, just vowels.

I know that people (living people) that are as involved with their bodies as people like weightlifters are give up a good amount of manual dexterity toward increasing their physical strength. I've seen body-builders lift cars over their heads but I've never seen them climb trees or catch rabbits. In a similar way, your dead have gained some resilience by shedding their material bodies, but have lost the ability to direct, particularize or make eloquent their gestures. Without a body, their intentions are activated ambiently and without any clear focus. As good as walking through walls and being able to see people naked without them seeing me sounds, and as uncontrollable and stupid and awkward as my body already is, I would still rather have than not have it.

In pornography (for sex that's not mine always provides the screenplay for all this) I'm always looking for my body or my body as it should be. I see living bodies that, above else, bulge. I see parts of them transgress and disperse into other parts, crashing into each other and making tangled, absurd messes. I see wide expanses of blank skin laid out for me to tattoo my name on. I see porn stars that I know are already dead but still there, still fucking. I see an arm that looks like mine but the wrist is always enough thicker. I see my little parakeet but a little parakeet that always turns into some monstrous, predatory vulture. I see my butt, a skinny butt, and I think my ass could look like that butt, at some obscure angle, that ass looks like my butt never could. My body's not funny. It's not even scary. It's already filled with the clutziness and inadequacies and shortcomings and ineffectiveness of the dead . . . Death, at this point, could only make me sexier. . . .

If you can use this paltry offering to mark another "x" on the wall of hell then go ahead. In death my body will, for once, have power. Aside from the outrageous smell and snarling strength of decomposition, it will have the power of the pathetic. Most folks are afraid of refuse and waste and cringe at the sight of shit or detached limbs or piled-up garbage. Fearsomeness is power and my power, my soiled and clammy patheticness through death will refuse to be dismantled. It is only dimly tinted by the boring distance between their living and my deadness because distance is, like living, easily surmounted. A ghost coming back to haunt is not nearly as scary as a lifeless, bloodless corpse. My power, through the distance of my corpse, folds in on itself, intertwines and resurfaces as a much more complex and treacherous matrix that expands in toward itself and multifoliates into some gothic and cannibalistic ellipse (like the infinity sign without saying anything as egregious as eternity). My body could certainly be that.

But of course, as always, my body is as stupid as me which is as stupid as a thief who breaks into a house just to have a look around. Death doesn't really have all that much more than I already have. Its ugly effects and theatrics are not that new to me. I'd still like to take a peak up Death's ass just to have a look around but it's useless to try to make a vacation out of it.

Dear Death, I know what you're up to so please stop bugging around me.

16

ONE. It's a nice view but I have the overwhelming urge to throw up. I'm on the sixteenth floor in a hospital room overlooking the east river and the southern skies of new york just as the planet spins into evening. My friend on the bed is lucky; in a room with two beds he got the one by the only window. The other guy lies in a tilt-a-bed on the other side of an ugly curtain with nothing to look at except life-sustaining chrome boxes and tubes and a big acrylic nightmare painting that looks like it was purchased from one of those Starving Artist Sales at the local Holiday Inn. It's of a woozy rain-filled street scene from some foreign city, maybe european. My friend has an identical painting on his portion of the wall only over the last few days I smuggled in a beginner's set of acrylics and when no one was looking I painted a fat monkey devouring lots of little humans. None of the hospital workers even noticed.

I never found out what's wrong with the guy in the other bed, he's maybe there for a week or two, then he disappears and is replaced by another desperate body. Sometimes they live, sometimes they die. When you don't know the person it is hard to know their pain. You're just left with your imagination trying to cull odd bits of personal history and sensation in order to approximate what it feels like to have just shit all over yourself and the clean white sheets of the bed.

The sky is a mobile of tiny colored lights wobbling through the threads of dusk. Any event would be appreciated at this moment, like one of the copters or small airplanes suddenly developing a small puff of smoke and flame in its tail and plummeting down among the canyon streets. That might erase for a moment the overwhelming smell of shit. It might distract me from the small panic sounds of the other guy behind the curtain honking like a suffocating goose. He's about ninety years old. I got a glimpse of him yesterday while visiting my friend. He's got a plastic oxygen mask strapped over his face so that when he screams it sounds like the voices you hear over a contraption made of two tin cans and a piece of wire. Calling long distance trying to get the operator. Someone in charge. Someone in authority. Someone who can make it all stop. With a pill, a solution, a knife, a needle, a word, a kiss, a smack, an embrace. Someone to erase the sliding world of fact. No such luck, the place is understaffed and as of this moment New York City has thirty-three thousand people homeless and dying of AIDS in the streets. Some senators breezed through a year ago gathering statistics on the problem but went away after being assured by city officials that the people in question were dying so fast from lack of health care that no one would notice an increase in visibility. The ones who died would make room for the ones coming up from behind.

About two blocks away is an enormous highrise building that blocks a portion of the southern view. At least three hundred little blue television screens are operating behind the windows simultaneously. Half of them are tuned to the same station, you can tell by the patterns of fluctuating light. Must be more war news. I wish this society would develop their vocabulary further in order to come up with a better term for what we call: *The Evening News*. In China they used to make people create paintings and songs entitled: "I'm So Happy When I Carry Manure Up The Hillside To The Commune." *The Evening News* is just as blatant. All they do is pop a handful of video frames out of the tv screen into our laps of a flag drifting by in the pale hands of a white zombie and everybody sends their kids to their deaths on the next tanker out. Lots of little yellow ribbons and stupid talk to comfort us as Junior gets his brains exploded overseas.

My friend on the bed never watches his tv which is attached to a robotic-looking arm made of chrome and gray metal protrud-

ing from the wall above his head. If he bothered to he would probably see a large crowd of kids in the desert of Kuwait talking
about how they were going to march straight through to Baghdad
and find a payphone and use it to call home. Then he would see
them writing out their wills on the customary supplied government forms. Or maybe he'd catch the video where the command-
ing instructor holds up a landmine and says, "If you step on one of
these there won't be nothing left of you to find. Just a red spray in
the air." Or the Fort Dix drill sergeant out of view of the rolling
cameras, "When ya see those towel-heads..."

But my friend on the bed doesn't appreciate the vision of
manure being shoveled out of the tv screen by elegantly dressed
newscasters. He'd be too weak to turn the channels and anyways
there's the question of whether or not he has dementia. Dementia
can be caused by the virus's activity in the brain. Dementia
means you see things like a visitor's face impaled with dozens of
nails or crawling with hundreds of flies and none of it surprises
you. So seeing Defense Secretary Dick Cheney looming up on the
telly with a weird lust in his eyes and bits of brain matter stuck in
the cracks of his teeth might accidentally be chalked up to the
effects of dementia.

The nurse finally arrives and behind the curtain I hear the
sounds of a body thumping, the sounds of cloth being rolled up, of
water splashing and covers being unfurled and tucked and eventually she leaves taking with her the smell of shit in a laundry
cart. I still fight the urge to puke. I've been fighting it all week.
Whenever I witness signs of physical distress I have to fight the
urge to bend over at the waist and empty out. It can be anything.
The bum on the corner with festering sores on his face. It could
be the moving skeleton I passed in the hall on the way in. Some
guy with Wasting Syndrome and CMV blindness who is leaning
precariously out of his wheelchair in the unattended hallway
searching in sightlessness for something he's lost. He's making
braying sounds. What he's looking for is beneath the wheels of his
chair. A tiny teddy bear with a collegiate outfit sewn to its body
and a little flag glued to its paw. I pick it up and notice it has saliva
and food matter stuck to its fur and I wonder if this is what civili-

zation boils down to. I place it in the guy's hands and he squeals at me, his eyes a dull gray like the bellies of small fish. I have to resist that urge to puke. It's upsetting but I realize I'm only nauseated by my own mortality.

My friend on the bed is waking. The hospital gown has pulled up along his torso in the motions of sleep revealing a blobby-looking penis and schools of cancer lesions twisting around his legs and abdomen. He opens his eyes too wide a couple of times and I hand him a bunch of flowers. "I see double," he says. "Twice as many flowers," I said.

TWO. This kid walks into my sleep he's maybe seventeen years old stretches out on a table says he's not feeling well. He may be naked or else wearing no shirt his hands behind his head. I can see a swollen lump pushing under the skin of his armpit. I place my hands on his stomach and chest and try to explain to him that he needs to be looked at by a doctor. In the shadows of this room in the cool blue light descending down the walls from the ceiling the kid is a very beautiful boy. He looks sad and shocked and closes his eyes like he doesn't want to know or like somehow he can shut it all out.

Later some guy appears in the place. He has an odd look about his face. He tries to make it known that he knows me or someone close to me. He leans in close has flat dull eyes like blue silvery coins behind his irises. I think it is the face of Death. I get agitated and disturbed and want to be left alone with the kid. Try to steer him away to some other location. He disappears for a moment and then reappears in the distance but far away isn't far enough. I turn and look at the kid on the table he looks about ten years old and water is pouring from his face.

THREE. It's a dark and wet concrete bunker, a basement that runs under the building from front to back. There is one other concrete staircase that is sealed off at the top by a street grate and you can hear the feet of pedestrians and spare parts of conversations floating down into the gloom. At a mid-point in the room you can do a 360-degree slow turn and see everything; the shaky alcoves built of cheap plywood, a long waist-high cement ledge where twenty-three guys could sit shoulder to shoulder if forced to, the darkened ledge in the back half-hidden by pipes and architectural supports, and the giant television set. It's one of the latest inventions from japan, the largest video monitor available and it is hooked and cabled into the wall, then further encased in a large sheet of Plexiglas in order to prevent the hands of some bored queen from fucking with the dials and switching the sex scenes into "Let's Make A Deal." The plexi is covered in scratches and handprints and smudges and discolored streaks of body fluids and at the moment the image fed from the vhs machine upstairs behind the front counter of the neighborhood sex shop is a bit on the blink. When the original film was transferred it was jumping the sprockets of the projector and now I'm watching images that fluctuate strobically up and down but by only a single centimeter. Each body or object or vista or close-up of eye, tongue, stiff dick and asshole is doubled and vibrating. Kind of pretty and psychedelic and no one is watching it anyways. There is a clump of three guys entwined on the long ledge. One of them is lying down leaning on one elbow with his head cradled in another guy's hand. The second guy is feeding the first guy his dick while a third guy is crouching down behind him pulling open the cheeks of his ass and licking his finger and poking at its bull's-eye. The shadows cast by their bodies cancel out the details necessary for making the vision interesting or decipherable beyond the basics. One of the guys, the one who looks like he's praying at an altar, turns and opens his mouth wide and gestures towards it. He nods at me but I turn away. He wouldn't understand. Too bad he can't see the virus in me, maybe it would rearrange something in him. It certainly did in me. When I found out I felt this abstract sensation: something like pulling off your skin and turning it inside out and then rearranging it so that when you pull it back on it feels like what it felt like before, only it isn't and only you know it. It's something almost imperceptible. I mean the first minute after being diagnosed you are forever separated from what one had come to view as one's life or living, the world outside the eyes. The calendar tracings of biographical continuity get kind of screwed up. It's like watching a movie suddenly and abruptly go in reverse a thousand miles a minute; like the entire landscape and horizon is pulling away from you in reverse in order to spell out a psychic separation. Like I said, he wouldn't understand and besides his hunger is giant. I once came in this place fresh out of visiting a friend in the hospital who was within a day or two of death and you wouldn't know there was an epidemic. At least forty people exploring every possible invention of sexual gesture and not a condom in sight. I had an idea where I would make a three-minute super-8 film of my dying friend's face with all its lesions and sightlessness and then take a super-8 projector and hook it up with copper cables to a car battery slung over my shoulder and walk back in here and project the film onto the dark walls above their heads. I didn't want to ruin their evening, just wanted to maybe keep their temporary worlds from narrowing down too far.

That momentary dick on the screen is actually quite beautiful. In its strobic movements there is a red and blue tinge to the vibrating outlines of things that reminds the eyes of childhood 3-D glasses and their accompanying comics and movies. Yet it's not just that. It's the doubling of things that are desirable including this hokey ranch cowboy, new boy on the fictional range, or am I confusing him with a secondary character, the park ranger out for a lonely walk in the burnt july countryside who impulsively decides to strip on the riverbank among sunbleached boulders and jerk off. He's thinking he's alone even though we can see the shadow of the camera perched on its tri-pod for one fleeting moment and he can only pretend that the camera is not there just like we are not there. In a moment the scene has changed and the ranger or the ranch cowboy is in a field of daisies and I'm thinking this must be a 60's film and he's laid down a blanket he forgot to bring his clothes where he left them scenes ago by the river-bank. With the hypnotically vibrating double-edged image it's almost overwhelming; he's in a sea of eyes, the daisy petals are like drawings of sumerian eyeballs or early north african stone carvings of the anatomy of the eye or a child's image of the portal to sleep and vision and it's millions of these blinding white petals probing the blue air around his blank white body and his taut belly stretches back as he arches his body he's on his knees fine gold-haired legs and one arm back palm to the ground to stop his gravitational fall and the veins in his neck run down to his corded arms and loop over his biceps. That hungry eye of mine follows the beautiful curve under his arm into that dark and moist spot and all of a sudden he is cumming and for a moment it wasn't possible to know that other than the exaggerated body language he throws off to let the viewer know he's having an orgasm that fictionally approximates the collision between a honda and a freight train. I notice in the psychedelic frenzy of vibrating blades of millions of daisies that his sperm is jetting out, spraying in shapes that mirror or approximate the petals in their whiteness and slant and the boy's body is jittering into doubles in the eyeball of this spectator and it's a moment where I wish I could slip through the physical dimensions of the tv screen like in some late-night outer limits episode and be consigned to occupy the space of that scene for all eternity; for the lengths of boring future history I would willingly lose myself in the kid's jumbled references.

FOUR. "I haven't seen my folks in almost five years. I don't know who the fuck it was but somebody told them I was shooting dope and they came down from connecticut to take me away. They piled all my belongings in a van and just before we left I asked my brother if I could take the van and go fill it full of gas and get a pack of cigarettes. He said: yes and I hopped in the van and just kept going til I ended up in Hawaii. I was there for a year, at first I was gonna live on the beach — I figured I was gonna die so I might as well die in a place that was beautiful. Then I came down with the first symptoms and now I got so much kaposi that I could be a firehouse dog. My leg they say is so bad that they might have to amputate it. You know me I'm probably more belligerent than ever more opinionated than ever. I drive a cab all night in philly all night every night. It took me eight months to get on medicaid but I got a couple of great doctors.

"Last week I had a slip and went out and bought a bag of coke and since there were all these needles lying around my place from doing interferon I shot the coke for five days and it felt good really great. These days I live with a couple of roommates, they work in the day I work in the night and so we hardly see each other. I bought a puppy the other day went to the shelter to get a cat and took one look at this puppy and see these spots on my wrists? Well that ain't nothin honey you oughta see my leg christ when the night's over after driving that cab my leg hurts so fucking bad I buy a pint of whiskey every morning and when I get home I sit down and uncap that bottle and just drink myself stupid. I don't care what anybody thinks I just drink myself to sleep. The interferon and other drugs I'm doing cost four hundred dollars a day actually four hundred bucks just for what I stick in my body with needles and my folks can't deal with my illness. They never saw me after I was diagnosed. Now I'm on my way up to Grand Central to see if I can catch a train and see them for the first time. Christmas, ya know.

"This restaurant used to be great but now they don't give you the automatic salad with the veal patties like they used to years ago I can't live without my salad.

"This girl I know in philly talked me into going swimming. I get so fucking lonely that's why I drink I mean I don't get dates like I used to no sex nothing no fun anymore. She talked me into going to the local indoor pool and I get up there on the diving board and I'm standing there getting ready to bounce and dive and as I look down I see this woman and she's got four kids in the pool and her eyes got like headlights and she takes one look at the lesions on my body and she starts screaming to her kids: OUTTA THE POOL OUTTA THE POOL and starts yanking them out of the water and all of a sudden there's all this fucking commotion around the edges of the pool with parents yanking their kids out left and right and my friend is rolling on the floor with laughter she can't even stand up she's laughing so hard so I take my dive and come up to the edge of the pool and say: what's so funny? and she says: I can't believe it—I gotta bring you with me every time I come here; this is the least crowded I ever saw this place in my life."

FIVE. He kept following me. Driving out of the parking lot a car pulled up behind mine. It had one headlight broken and the driver flashed his brights for a moment blinding me as I studied the dark spot of his windshield through my rearview mirror for some smudged view of his face. He looked okay from what I could tell but I ignored him and his signals. He was persistent though following me through town at all the stop signs and red lights either flashing his brights in my eyes or else dimly nodding at me over and over. I acted indifferent but he followed me to where I coasted up to the curb in front of the gray clapboard house I was staying in under the heavy trees. The babysitter the family had hired was watching tv a soft bluewhite glow pulsing through the porch windows. I got out of my car and walked back to his caught in the full blaze of headlights from a passing car. I heard his voice before I really saw his face. "What ya up to?" The car passed everything on the street disappeared again and I leaned against the driver's side of the door his window down. "Oh, I don't know. . . it's hard to explain," I said looking around me for signs of life. "You married?" he asked. "No. I got other problems. Medical ones," I said. I noticed he was jerking off in the darkness of his seat. He asked me to take my shirt off so he could look at my chest. I said no thinking of the neighbors or babysitter looking out the windows. His shirt was open to the last couple of buttons and in the glow of distant porch lights his chest muscles looked rounded and divided by a little hair growing down towards the belly. I reached in and slid my hands slowly over his body under the folds of his shirt under his arms around his shoulders and he gasped and arched his head back and his hips bucked upwards and a stream of white semen whiter than his skin jetted across his stomach and fingers. When I got inside the house on the second floor the child of the family was asleep in the hall on the floor outside his room looking like he'd fallen off a sled.

SIX. I had an odd sleep last night. I felt like I was lying in the motel room for hours half awake or maybe I was just dreaming that I was half awake. In some part of my sleep I saw this fat little white worm, a grub-like thing that was no bigger than a quarter of an inch. When I leaned very close to it, my eye just centimeters above it I could see every detail of the ridges of its flesh. It was a meat eater. It had fastened onto what looked like an inch-long fetal creature. What the worm had latched onto looked like a goat fetus, or maybe a ram fetus. It had large looping horns protruding from its head. Keep in mind that this thing was a couple inches in length. The whole thing was white, fetal in appearance, its horns were translucent like fingernails. The grub was beginning to eat it and I pulled it off. It became very agitated and angry and tried to start eating my fingers. I threw it onto the ground but there was yet another one and it was crawling towards some other fetal-looking thing, what appeared to be a mouse fetus or something. I smacked it really hard. Picked it up and threw it down but my actions didn't kill it. My location was a wet dark hillside around dawn or dusk with a little light drifting over the landscape. Looking around I realized that the entire contents of a biology lab or pet shop had been dumped by somebody on the ground. Maybe I had stolen everything. There were big black tarantulas, all sorts of lizards, some small mammals and bugs and frogs and snake things. They're lying on the ground in all this moist earth and leaves among tree branches, roots and grass stalks. At some point this big black tarantula was crawling around, really a blue-black and the size of a catcher's mitt. It made a little jump like it had seized something. I looked closely and saw it was eating an extraordinarily beautiful monitor lizard, a baby one. The spider didn't scare me; my sense of anxiety came from mixing the species. They all seemed to have come from different countries and were now thrown accidently together by research or something. I pushed at the spider, picked it up and tried to unfasten its mandibles from the belly of the lizard. Someone else was with me; I handed them the spider and said, "Take it somewhere else or put it in something until I figure out what I'm doing." The person threw the spider on the ground in a rough manner. I said, "Don't do that — you'll kill it." If you drop a tarantula from a height higher than five inches its abdomen will burst.

SEVEN. Fevers. I wake up these mornings feeling wet like something of my soul, my memories, is seeping out the back of my head into the cloth and stuffing of the pillows. I woke up earlier with an intense nausea and one of those headaches that lodge behind the eyes and in the top of the spine. I guess it's from dehydration or something. I turned on the television to try and get some focus outside my illness. Every station was filled with half-hour commercials disguised as talk shows in which failed or boring low-grade tv actors and actresses talk about how to whiten your teeth or raise your investment earnings or shake the extra pounds from your bones. I am convinced I am from another planet after watching these things for more than a minute. One station had a full close-up of a woman's face, middle-aged, saying, "People talk about a sensation they've experienced when they are close to death where their entire lives pass before their eyes. Well, it is the same, you experience a similar moment when you are about to kill someone. You look at that person and see something in the moment before you kill them. You see his home, his family, his childhood, his hopes and beliefs, his sorrows and his joys; all this passes before you in a flash." I didn't know what she was making these references for but then the confusion was cleared when a video was played of Whitney Houston singing the star spangled banner. I tried to figure out where at five in the morning I could run and buy an american flag. My head hurt so bad I had to get out of bed and stand upright in order to ease the pressure. Gosh, the way her voice quavered when she got to the part about the bombs, waving flag and freedom. I went into the bathroom and finally threw up. I came back into the living room, yanked open the window and leaned out above the dark streets and screamed, "I FEEL LIKE THERE IS A SOMETHING IN MY BLOOD AND IT'S TRYING TO KILL ME."

EIGHT. It's that face. I knew I'd seen it before. How do I describe this? I'm standing in the lobby of a movie theatre surrounded by crowds of people waiting to enter the auditorium to watch a film about a bunch of teenagers and a dead body and codes of teenage silence. It's the end of the previous show and the doors are flung open and hundreds of people are pouring out towards the exits.

Suddenly that face. It's one anonymous face in the crowd that tips the switch in the back of my head. I froze and the face became magnified. It expanded in size until it was five feet tall and disembodied and floating in the darkness of the open doors. Credits rolled by its left ear further back in the emptying theatre. I guess he froze too. It was a pale gray color with fastidiously combed hair plastered down around the skull. Thin lips bloodless and tight. His eyes were colorless and they widened for a fraction of a moment. We both stood there trying to uncoil each other's private histories and solve the dislocation of familiarity. Was it something located in a past desire or repulsion? When I noticed his suit and his hands, palms back and manicured nails, I remembered. He was moving suddenly. He brushed by me with a hissing sound and went down a staircase towards the bathrooms throwing a dead glance over his shoulder. I didn't know if he expected me to follow; I was actually trembling and it took me a moment to get my legs moving through the doorway into the theatre to look for a seat.

I had been drugged, tossed out a second-story window, strangled, smacked in my head with a slab of marble, almost stabbed four times, punched in the face at least seventeen times, beat about my body too many times to recount, almost completely suffocated, and woken up once tied to a hotel bed with my head over the side all the blood rushed down into it making it feel like it was going to explode, all this before I turned fifteen. I chalked it up to adventure or the risks of being a kid prostitute in new york city. At that point in my life dying didn't mean anything to me other than a big drag. I had mixed feelings about death. When I was trying to get enough money up to eat or find a place to sleep for the night, death actually seemed attractive, an alternative. I would go without changing my clothes or bathing for months at a time. I could see my reflection in the legs of my pants if I bent close to them. Periodically if I had a surplus of money from spreading my legs in seven dollar hotels on eighth avenue I would walk into the Port Authority bus terminal and look at all the various names of towns painted on the glass windows of the ticket booths. I'd choose one that suggested bodies of water and then buy a ticket, get on the bus and ride it for as long as it took till I spotted a lake or pond in the countryside. I'd then ask the bus driver to let me off, usually having to argue with him because it wasn't a scheduled stop. After the bus continued on its way I would walk across the field and into the water until I was up to my neck. I never bothered to take my shoes or clothes off. I would drift and float around for hours and then hike back to the road and hitch a ride to a bus stop or all the way back into the city.

That face. Maybe it was the qualities of light or lack of it in the lobby as the door swung open and people were exiting before the end of the film leader spun out from the projector. Maybe it was the color of his flesh, the look of no oxygen, the look of antici-pation or fear, the complexion of anticipation.

I remember that night fifteen years earlier. I had spent the later part of the afternoon paddling around this small pond, push-ing my face underwater and among the shore grass looking for signs of life. It was rapidly turning to dusk and I was wet and feeling cold. The town was too small to offer much evening traffic so it was hard to get a ride. I didn't really know where I was. I was gray inside my head and wishing that killing myself was an effort-less act. It's hard to remember the drift.

Those eyes. That face gray and floating disembodied in the dark of the open window. A small beat-up red pick-up truck coasted to a stop along the side of the road. A shock of the pale hand floating up from the shadows of the seat and spinning softly in the air. He was waving me into the truck. I remember thinking his skin was fake, like a semi-translucent latex. I asked him how far he was going. "Oh, a ways." Thin tight voice layered with a friendliness I couldn't hook into. We drove for a while in silence and I looked out the side window at all the illuminated houses and occasional glimpses of people exiting cars in driveways or interacting with others in private communications. A stray dog running along the highway in a small panic. He said he worked in a bank in the city. That depressed me for some reason, maybe the formality of it that translated into an image of years and years of writing in ledgers and stale cups of coffee and dealing with peo-ple in need. At some point he had his dick out and stared out through the windshield at the beacons of light illuminating the dark roadway. He steered with one hand and jerked off with the other. I was leaning against the door and didn't answer when he murmured something about this place he knew where we could go. After a while he make a left turn down a gravel and dirt road winding up through a forest over small hills. I remember moths and bugs diving into the headlights, a small wood sign with a boy scout symbol on it, then some scattered cabins. The sound of lake water in the near distance.

He got out of the driver's seat and pulled open the passenger door I was seated behind. "Squat down and make it squirt." I didn't move. He had shut the engine off and the headlights as well, just soft wavy clouds of darkness that were occupied by fir trees. "Get out." I felt suddenly much more tired than I ever remember feeling. I swung my legs out from the seat and stood in front of him with my hands in my pockets. A wind was coming up and it was starting to bring with it a light rain. He took me by the arm and led me to the back of the truck and turned a metal latch and swung up on the back door of the camper. One of his hands floated up to my face and then encircled the back of my neck and I realized I was being propelled forward towards the black interior of the camper. I crawled obediently inside, it was loaded with blankets and sleeping bags and boxes of indecipherable stuff. It was kind of moist and smelled like earth and grease. He climbed in behind me and pulled the door shut. Dark gray are the only words for the light through the windows; everything was more reduced to smells and the sound of trees and the squeak of his shoes against the metal parts of the floor. I lay down and curled up on a mass of smelly cloth. I could see his silhouette half-rise before me, blocking out the minimal light and then dropping to my side. The sound of a zipper opening. His hand on my neck again. Pulling. "I want to go home," I said. "What are you talking about?" I realized his head was further back in the truck than I had thought. I couldn't see anything. The rain was coming down hard; sheets of water making the dimness more dark. "I don't know," I said, wondering where I would go even if I got out of the truck without him stopping me. "You like it in your ass?" "No."

"Good," he said and then hit me. Very hard.

I'm blind to the world and he's turning me over and over and over. Where am I? In a muddy field in the back of a stranger's truck and the truck is backed up to a fence and the stranger has put his full weight on my back and I feel like I'm in motion like something flung out of a giant slingshot. A pale length of rope hastily torn out of a wet cardboard box and wrapped around my hands pulled behind my back. I'm on my belly and if I yelled or hollered the only thing to hear me is the dead house miles back on the road dark and empty. Or the handful of run-down shuttered factories on the main road. He's pulling my hair, yanking my head back so his face appears upside down floating before mine and he's smiling. But the smile looks like a frown, it's upside down and he leans in and kisses both my eyes. The windows have fogged up and he opened one slightly and I can hear the occasional whine of insects. He's slapping my bare butt and driving his tongue into my ear and running it down the line of my neck and turning me over and over periodically. I'm overwhelmed by the smell of wet metal and the musky thickness of the cloth when my face is ground into a blanket or sleeping bag what's he doing kneeling on my head I ain't no doll with replaceable body parts. He's stuffing a rolled-up blanket beneath my naked body forcing my ass up into the air I can't feel my hands anymore all the circulation is gone. Funny how everything all my life moved excruciatingly slow until this moment and now I'm just begging for it to stop. He giggles and disappears from the truck. I hear the sound of shoes on the grit and wetness of the road and the camper dips as he climbs back in. He lies on top of me I'd feel fucking cold but his body is generating intense heat. His shirt's off and his pants are down or gone. He starts slamming his body down on top of mine periodically his arm curving around my face, "Lick that bicep." His arm pulls back, fingers shove something in my mouth; it's a wad of mud and sand. He treats me like he owns me. I'm stuck in a drift lost of hope or anything familiar. Maybe now I'll get relief, maybe he'll crush my skull or strangle me. Suddenly I recall something from earlier when he loosened my belt and dragged my pants down to my calves and smacked me as hard as he could and it hurt so bad I tried to make it sexual I tried to imagine it was gentle or that he was somebody sexy or that I was a mile away walking in the opposite direction. "Oh hit me," I said trying to act like I was into it so maybe he'd get bored. Turning over and over and over what the fuck is he doing that for? He lunges and reaches far into the darkness of the truck and I hear a container of liquid, sounds like a metal container and liquid sounds the image of lighter fluid or gasoline went through my mind. Is this it? I could see the flames; I could see my body being turned over by campers looking like a side of beef left too long in the fire, black and charred with bones poking out of it. I felt the squirt of liquid all over my ass, a memory smell from childhood flooding the truck. Baby oil. I just want to die, I just want to die, I just want to die — if I say it often enough will I lose my fear of his hands tightening around my throat? I'm sinking in dark pools of atmosphere and his palm is sliding around the small of my back, into the crack of my ass cheeks. "Oh what a gift you're giving me," he mumbles. He grabs my tied arms pressing his full weight on them pinning my elbows at an outrageous angle to the cold metal floor and shoves his dick into me. "Ow." He's biting my cheek. Slap. Slap. Burying his face in my neck and biting again. I'm still sinking and his bites and slaps are so specific I think he hasn't lost control just four fingers in my mouth weight holding me down kissing my eyes breathing hard in my ear pumping like a machine, "You like that steady rhythm?" "Uh." Rain sounds on the truck roof and windows and wet mud the only returnable answers.

17

Worsewick Hot Springs was nothing fancy. Somebody put some boards across the creek. That was it.

The boards dammed up the creek enough to form a huge bathtub there, and the creek flowed over the top of the boards, invited like a postcard to the ocean a thousand miles away.

As I said Worsewick was nothing fancy, not like the places where the swells go. There were no buildings around. We saw an old shoe lying by the tub.

The hot springs came down off a hill and where they flowed there was a bright orange scum through the sagebrush. The hot springs flowed into the creek right there at the tub and that's where it was nice.

We parked our car on the dirt road and went down and took off our clothes, then we took off the baby's clothes, and the deer-flies had at us until we got into the water, and then they stopped.

There was a green slime growing around the edges of the tub and there were dozens of dead fish floating in our bath. Their bodies had been turned white by death, like frost on iron doors. Their eyes were large and stiff.

The fish had made the mistake of going down the creek too far and ending up in hot water, singing, "When you lose your money, learn to lose."

We played and relaxed in the water. The green slime and the dead fish played and relaxed with us and flowed out over us and entwined themselves about us.

Splashing around in that hot water with my woman, I began to get ideas, as they say. After a while I placed by body in such a position in the water that the baby could not see my hard-on.

I did this by going deeper and deeper in the water, like a dinosaur, and letting the green slime and dead fish cover me over.

My woman took the baby out of the water and gave her a bottle and put her back in the car. The baby was tired. It was *really* time for her to take a nap.

My woman took a blanket out of the car and covered up the windows that faced the hot springs. She put the blanket on top of the car and then lay rocks on the blanket to hold it in place. I remember her standing there by the car.

Then she came back to the water, and the deerflies were at her, and then it was my turn. After a while she said, "I don't have my diaphragm with me and besides it wouldn't work in the water, anyway. I think it's a good idea if you don't come inside me. What do you think?"

I thought this over and said all right. I didn't want any more kids for a long time. The green slime and dead fish were all about our bodies.

I remember a dead fish floated under her neck. I waited for it to come up on the other side, and it came up on the other side.

Worsewick was nothing fancy.

Then I came, and just cleared her in a split second like an airplane in the movies, pulling out of a nosedive and sailing over the roof of a school.

My sperm came out into the water, unaccustomed to the light, and instantly it became a misty, stringy kind of thing and swirled out like a falling star, and I saw a dead fish come forward and float into my sperm, bending it in the middle. His eyes were stiff like iron.

18

Seventeen years later I sat down on a rock. It was under a tree next to an old abandoned shack that had a sheriff's notice nailed like a funeral wreath to the front door.

NO TRESPASSING

4/17 OF A HAIKU

Many rivers had flowed past those seventeen years, and thousands of trout, and now beside the highway and the sheriff's notice flowed yet another river, the Klamath, and I was trying to get thirty-five miles downstream to Steelhead, the place where I was staying.

It was all very simple. No one would stop and pick me up even though I was carrying fishing tackle. People usually stop and pick up a fisherman. I had to wait three hours for a ride.

The sun was like a huge fifty-cent piece that someone had poured kerosene on and then had lit with a match and said, "Here, hold this while I go get a newspaper," and put the coin in my hand, but never came back.

I had walked for miles and miles until I came to the rock under the tree and sat down. Every time a car would come by, about once every ten minutes, I would get up and stick out my thumb as if it were a bunch of bananas and then sit back down on the rock again.

The old shack had a tin roof colored reddish by years of wear, like a hat worn under the guillotine. A corner of the roof was loose and a hot wind blew down the river and the loose corner clanged in the wind.

A car went by. An old couple. The car almost swerved off the road and into the river. I guess they didn't see many hitchhikers up there. The car went around the corner with both of them looking back at me.

I had nothing else to do, so I caught salmon flies in my landing net. I made up my own game. It went like this: I couldn't chase after them. I had to let them fly to me. It was something to do with my mind. I caught six.

A little ways up from the shack was an outhouse with its door flung violently open. The inside of the outhouse was exposed like a human face and the outhouse seemed to say, "The old guy who built me crapped in here 9,745 times and he's dead now and I don't want anyone else to touch me. He was a good guy. He built me with loving care. Leave me alone. I'm a monument now to a good ass gone under. There's no mystery here. That's why the door's open. If you have to crap, go in the bushes like the deer."

"Fuck you," I said to the outhouse. "All I want is a ride down the river."

———————————————

19

I was driving to Las Vegas to tell my sister that I'd had Mother's respirator unplugged. Four bald men in the convertible in front of me were picking the scabs off their sunburnt heads and flicking them onto the road. I had to swerve to avoid riding over one of the oozy crusts of blood and going into an uncontrollable skid. I maneuvered the best I could in my boxy Korean import but my mind was elsewhere. I hadn't eaten for days. I was famished. Suddenly as I reached the crest of a hill, emerging from the fog, there was a bright neon sign flashing on and off that read: FOIE GRAS AND HARICOTS VERTS NEXT EXIT. I checked the guidebook and it said: *Excellent food, malevolent ambience.* I'd been habitually abusing an illegal growth hormone extracted from the pituitary glands of human corpses and I felt as if I were drowning in excremental filthiness but the prospect of having something good to eat cheered me up. I asked the waitress about the soup du jour and she said that it was primordial soup — which is ammonia and methane mixed with ocean water in the presence of lightning. Oh I'll take a tureen of that embryonic broth, I say, constraint giving way to exuberance — but as soon as she vanished my spirit immediately sags because the ambience is so malevolent. The bouncers are hassling some youngsters who want drinks — instead of simply carding the kids, they give them radiocarbon tests, using traces of carbon 14 to determine how old they are — and also there's a young wise guy from Texas A&M at a table near mine who asks for freshly ground Rolaids on his fettuccine and two waiters viciously work him over with heavy bludgeon-sized pepper mills, so I get right back into my car and narcissistically comb my thick jet-black hair in the rearview mirror and I check the guidebook. There's an inn nearby — it's called Little Bo Peep's — its habitues are shepherds. And after a long day of herding, shearing, panpipe playing, muse invoking, and conversing in eclogues, it's Miller time, and Bo Peep's is packed with rustic swains who've left their flocks and sunlit, idealized arcadia behind for the more pungent charms of hard-core social intercourse. Everyone's favorite waitress is Kikugoro. She wears a pale-blue silk kimono and a brocade obi of gold and silver chrysanthemums with a small fan tucked into its folds, her face is painted and powdered to a porcelain white. A cowboy from south of the border orders a "Biggu Makku." But Kikugoro says, "This is not Makudonarudo." She takes a long cylinder of gallium arsenide crystal and slices him a thin wafer which she serves with soy sauce, wasabi, pickled ginger, and daikon. "Conducts electrons ten times faster than sili-con...taste good, gaucho-*san*, you eat," she says, bowing.

My sister is the beautiful day. Oh beautiful day, my sister, wipe my nose, swaddle me in fresh-smelling garments. I nurse at the adamantine nipple of the beautiful day, I quaff the milk of the beautiful day, and for the first time since 1956, I cheese on the shoulder of the beautiful day. Oh beautiful day, wash me in your lake of cloudless azure. I have overdosed on television, I am unresponsive and cyanotic, revive me in your shower of gelid light and walk me through your piazza which is made of elegant slabs of time. Oh beautiful day, kiss me. Your mouth is the Columbus Day. You are the menthol of autumn. My lungs cannot quench their thirst for you. Resuscitate me — I will never exhale your tonic gasses. Inflate me so that I may rise into the sky and mourn the monotonous topography of my life. Oh beautiful day, my sister, wipe my nose and adorn me in your finery. Let us lunch alfresco. Your club sandwiches are made of mulch and wind perfumed with newsprint. Your frilly toothpicks are the deciduous trees of school days.

I was an infinitely hot and dense dot. So begins the autobiography of a feral child who was raised by huge and lurid puppets. An autobiography written wearing wrist weights. It ends with these words: A car drives through a puddle of sperm, sweat, and contraceptive jelly, splattering the great chopsocky vigilante from Hong Kong. Inside, two acephalic sardines in mustard sauce are asleep in the rank darkness of their tin container. Suddenly, the swinging doors burst open and a mesomorphic cyborg walks in and whips out a 35-lb. phallus made of corrosion-resistant nickel-base alloy and he begins to stroke it sullenly, his eyes half shut. It's got a metal-oxide membrane for absolute submicron filtration of petrochemical fluids. It can ejaculate herbicides, sulfuric acid, tar glue, you name it. At the end of the bar, a woman whose album-length poem about temporomandibular joint dysfunction (TMJ) had won a Grammy for best spoken-word recording is gently slowly ritually rubbing copper hexafluoroacetylacetone into her clitoris as she watches the hunk with the non-Euclidian features shoot a glob of dehydrogenated ethylbenzene 3,900 miles towards the Arctic archipelago, eventually raining down upon a fiord on Baffin Bay. Outside, a basketball plunges from the sky, killing a dog. At a county fair, a huge and hairy man in mud-caked blue overalls, surrounded by a crowd of retarded teenagers, swings a sledgehammer above his head with brawny keloidal arms and then brings it down with all his brute force on a tofu-burger on a flowery paper plate. A lizard licks the dew from the stamen of a stunted crocus. Rivets and girders float above the telekinetic construction works. The testicular voice of Barry White emanates from some occult source within the laundry room. As I chugalug a glass of tap water milky with contaminants, I realize that my mind is being drained of its contents and refilled with the beliefs of the most mission-oriented, can-do feral child ever raised by huge lurid puppets. I am the voice . . . the voice from beyond and the voice from within — can you hear me? Yes. I speak to you and you only — is that clear? Yes, master. To whom do I speak? To me and me only. Is "happy" the appropriate epithet for someone who experiences each moment as if he were being alternately flayed alive and tickled to death? No, master.

In addition to the growth hormone extracted from the glands of human corpses, I was using anabolic steroids, tissue regeneration compounds, granulocyte-macrophage colony-stimulating factor (GM-CSF) — a substance used to stimulate growth of certain vital blood cells in radiation victims — and a nasal spray of neuropeptides that accelerates the release of pituitary hormones and I was getting larger and larger and my food bills were becoming enormous. So I went on a TV game show in the hopes of raising cash. This was my question, for $250,000 in cash and prizes: If the Pacific Ocean were filled with gin, what would be, in terms of proportionate volume, the proper lake of vermouth necessary to achieve a dry martini? I said Lake Ontario — but the answer was the Caspian Sea which is called a sea but is a lake by definition. I had failed. I had humiliated my family and disgraced the kung fu masters of the Shaolin temple. I stared balefully out into the studio audience which was chanting something that sounded like "dork." I'm in my car. I'm high on Sinutab. And I'm driving anywhere. The vector of my movement from a given point is isotropic — meaning that all possible directions are equally probable. I end up at a squalid little dive somewhere in Vegas maybe Reno maybe Tahoe. I don't know . . . but there she is. I can't tell if she's a human or a fifth-generation gynemorphic android and I don't care. I crack open an ampule of mating pheromone and let it waft across the bar, as I sip my drink, a methyl isocyanate on the rocks — methyl isocyanate is the substance which killed more than 2,000 people when it leaked in Bhopal, India, but thanks to my weight training, aerobic workouts, and a low-fat fiber-rich diet, the stuff has no effect on me. Sure enough she strolls over and occupies the stool next to mine. After a few moments of silence, I make the first move: We're all larval psychotics and have been since the age of two, I say, spitting an ice cube back into my glass. She moves closer to me. At this range, the downy cilia-like hairs that trickle from her navel remind me of the fractal ferns produced by injecting dyed water into an aqueous polymer solution, and I tell her so. She looks into my eyes: You have the glibness, superficial charm, grandiosity, lack of guilt, shallow feelings, impulsiveness, and lack of realistic long-term plans that excite me right now, she says, moving even closer. We feed on the same prey species, I growl. My lips are now one angstrom unit from her lips, which is one ten-billionth of a meter. I begin to kiss her but she turns her head away. Don't good little boys who finish all their vegetables get dessert? I ask. I can't kiss you, we're monozygotic replicants — we share 100% of our genetic material. My head spins. You are the beautiful day, I exclaim, your breath is a zephyr of eucalyptus that does a pas de bouree across the Sea of Galilee. Thanks, she says, but we can't go back to my house and make love because monozygotic incest is forbidden by the elders. What if I said I could change all that. . . . What if I said that I had a miniature shotgun that blasts gene fragments into the cells of living organisms, altering their genetic matrices so that a monozygotic replicant would no longer be a monozygotic replicant and she could then make love to a muscleman without transgressing the incest taboo, I say, opening my shirt and exposing the device which I had stuck in the waistband of my black jeans. How'd you get that thing? she gasps, ogling its thick fiber-reinforced plastic barrel and the Uzi-Biotech logo embossed on the magazine which held two cartridges of gelated recombinant DNA. I got it for Christmas. . . . Do you have any last words before I scramble your chromosomes, I say, taking aim. Yes, she says, you first. I put the barrel to my heart. These are my last words: When I emerged from my mother's uterus I was the size of a chicken bouillon cube and Father said to the obstetrician: I realize that at this stage it's difficult to prognosticate his chances for a productive future, but if he's going to remain six-sided and 0.4 grams for the rest of his life, then euthanasia's our best bet. But Mother, who only milliseconds before was in the very throes of labor, had already slipped on her muumuu and espadrilles and was puffing on a Marlboro: No pimple-faced simp two months out of Guadalajara is going to dissolve this helpless little hexahedron in a mug of boiling water, she said, as a nurse managed with acrobatic desperation to slide a suture basin under the long ash of her cigarette which she'd consumed in one furiously deep drag. These are my last words: My fear of being bullied and humiliated stems from an incident that occurred many years ago in a diner. A 500-lb. man seated next to me at the counter was proving that one particular paper towel was more absorbent than another brand. His face was swollen and covered with patches of hectic red. He spilled my glass of chocolate milk on the counter and then sopped it up with one paper towel and then with the other. With each wipe of the counter the sweep of his huge dimpled arm became wider and wider until he was repeatedly smashing his flattened hand and the saturated towel into my chest. There was an interminable cadence to the blows I endured. And instead of assistance from other patrons at the counter, I received their derision, their sneering laughter. But now look at me! I am a terrible god. When I enter the forest the mightiest oaks blanch and tremble. All rustling, chirping, growling, and buzzing cease, purling brooks become still. This is all because of my tremendous muscularity... which is the result of the hours of hard work that I put in at the gym and the strict dietary regimen to which I adhere. When I enter the forest the birds become incontinent with fear so there's this torrential downpour of shit from the trees. And I stride through — my whistle is like an earsplitting fife being played by a lunatic with a bloody bandage around his head. And the sunlight, rent into an incoherence of blazing vectors, illuminates me: a shimmering, serrated monster!

20

the human bomb is ticking

the handsome blond robotic bomb with the gorgeous pecs and the
     cleft in his chin and the cute mustache is purring: tick tock
     tick tock tick tock

he puts a pinch of smokeless tobacco between his cheek and gum
     and watches a monarch butterfly mince gingerly across the
     hot hood of his idling chevy malibu

and little lovely winged electric razors hover about his head,
     gently kissing it until he is bald—and he dreams of john
     audubon and his lovely watercolor hummingbirds and his
     lonely watercolor chrysanthemums—though, unbeknownst
     to the human bomb, the ceramic cranium developed for him
     by japanese high-tech ceramics engineers to protect his
     brain is beginning to crack, so that really his watercolor
     dream of john audubon is not a dream at all but an aberrant
     pattern of electrical discharge generated by moisture seep-
     ing through the fissures in his glazed skull

and unbeknownst to the human bomb, he's been tampered with
     by terrorists who've rigged his detonator to his prostate
     gland, so the instant he ejaculates—*boom*!

it is autumn

and i am remembering autumn nights long ago when we watched
     those early episodes in which the handsome human bomb
     was motionlessly posed in the men's department at macy's in
     a van heusen cream-colored button-down, pierre cardin pin-

dot lamb's wool tie, a nut brown ralph lauren shetland wool
sweater, stanley blacker corduroy sport coat, and bass wee-
jun tassel-front brown leather slip-ons regularly $68 now on
sale for $54.40

you were just a flag twirler at pocahontas high in mahwah

it was homecoming night when i met you

i remember you giggling shyly at the seniors bobbing for veal
medallions in a metal basin of marsala sauce

you smelled of lilacs

that night we learned that ecstasy means the collapse of time

past present future perceived in a single instant

you were watching the trajectory of your own words as they left
your mouth

words which disappeared into the horizon

words which, due to the curvature of space, returned many years
later like murmuring boomerangs to your ear

you looked like an italian starlet — jet-black hair in a thick braid
down your back, sloe-eyes set deeply above high cheekbones,
olive complexion, full sensuous lips, the strap of your night-
gown fallen languorously off your shoulder, mascara
smeared, your eyelids heavy with drowsiness, your hair now
spread across the pillow like a trellis of vines, your voice low
and husky, your breath still redolent of anisette

and tonight as we watch television on the porch

your buckteeth seem shellacked in the cadmium light of the har-
vest moon

look at the screen

that's me with the amulets and anaconda pelts and the saucer-
size lip plug distending my mouth

that's me crouched in the backseat of the human bomb's chevy
malibu with his chubby friend ulrike grunebaum

though, without the proper software, ulrike grunebaum is like
mrs. potato head — without eyes, ears, nose, or mouth, without id or libido, without creed or lineage — a featureless and
vacant globe of flesh

but with the proper software, she is ulrike grunebaum, the chill-
ingly eloquent marxist ideologue and machiavellian techno-

crat in a gray three-piece suit and red necktie, ruthlessly
purging the upper echelons of her ruling politburo

with the proper software, she is ulrike grunebaum, executive
curator of the jimi hendrix museum in baden-baden

and with the proper software — with a twist of the joystick — she is
ulrike grunebaum, the hamburg erotic film queen whose
screen credits include *smell me tomorrow, the edible fixation,
we'll be nude at noon,* and *the odyssey of gomer*

we're taste-testing four varieties of lebanese halvah: druse, phalangist, sunni, and shiite

the flecks of shrapnel in the phalangist halvah give it an unusu-
ally nutty flavor

we're doing our cellulite exercises; we're doing the nine or ten
beautifully firming things you can do for your derriere

they're showing the video we made together for mtv in which i
play the naughty con ed man who's been discovered by ulrike
rummaging through her laundry hamper, sniffing her bras-
sieres, and ulrike wraps her prehensile eyelashes around my
delicate reed of a penis and slowly and erotically strangles it
until its head is the brilliant red of autumn sumac leaves

when i put my ear against ulrike's temple i can glean her
thoughts — because her thoughts are transmitted in the
morse code of her pulsing arteries

the human bomb throws his hot dog in the bushes

i'm about to say something horrible, something horribly unchris-
tian . . . and please don't start singing, because no amount of
mouthwash can camouflage the foul breath of hymn-singing
christians . . .

this is my horrible statement: there's mustard in the bushes

your eyes follow the squiggle of yellow mustard to an ant who's
about to be squashed beneath a shiny tooled-leather tony
lama cowboy boot and the ant looks directly into the camera
and says in yiddish with english subtitles, "i want to live as
much as you do" — and this image traumatizes the country in
the 1980s as much as the image of my head rolling from the
guillotine saying, "i'm sorry, mommy, i'll be good" trauma-

tized the country in the 1960s

i am on every channel and that infuriates you

that i have the ability to jump out of the television screen, burrow into your uterus, and emerge nine months later tan and rested bugs you very much

you're using the violent vocabulary of the u.s.a., you're violently chewing your cheez doodles and flicking the remote control

a computer programmer and mother of two from bethesda, maryland, puts her fingers through the holes in my head and bowls me

i'm rolling through roanoke, city of rheumatism and alzheimer's disease; through memphis, city of ulcerated tongues and saliva turned bitter and glutinous; through pine bluff, whose inhabitants store the ashes of their cremated dead in those white chardboard cartons with thin metal handles made for chinese takeout food; through shreveport, whose population lacks the enzyme necessary to break down spaghetti

I appear on the phil donahue show with other children of parents who'd had unsuccessful tubal ligations and vasectomies

my path connects every dot in texas

—oh dear, i'm quite lost; kind sir, can you tell me where i am?

—my, you're a peculiar sight, young man, you're balding but so pretty, are you gay?

—no, sir, i have a cute girlfriend at home who is waiting for me, please tell me where i am and lend me a quarter so i can call home and reassure my sweetheart that i have not been slain

—i am ordinarily the very soul of munificence, young friend, but today you find me rather strapped for cash or coin...perhaps in lieu of this phone call you will retire with me to a public lavatory and i will initiate you into the splendors of synchronized swimming

—i repeat with all respect, sir, that i am not homosexual; who are you, sir, and...who are you?

—i am not an octopus or a hen

—that i can see...nor a crayfish

(later)

— things didn't, did they? i mean turn out the way you expected

— no, i was incapable of accepting my mother's death and i frantically embraced fundamentalist judaism because i refused to accept a world in which people were so completely vulnerable and so capriciously and arbitrarily victimized, i refused to endorse the purposelessness and the randomness and i rushed into the arms of the paternalistic teleological belief system of my ancestors, of my parents, the very same judaism i'd so contemptuously eschewed my whole life — but even my newfound jewishness was fugitive

— how tall were you before your mother passed away?

— i was five-seven

— and the day after your mother passed away?

— four-one

— and today?

— today i am eight inches in diameter

— it sounds like you're going to disappear

— no, i'm in a perpetual state of contraction and expansion; now i'm contracting and just as i'm about to become smaller than anything, smaller than even the most infinitesimal subatomic particle, i'll begin to expand and i'll expand and expand and expand until there's literally no more room for me in the universe and my head is knocking against the ceiling of the space-time continuum and then i'll start to contract again and so on and so forth

i'm rolling down the pacific coast of south america, but i never make it to tierra del fuego

i'm a gutter ball

i was made in hong kong

i have reached a level of unparalleled ugliness — revolting bloated oily ugliness which has metastasized across every square inch of my body

sexual relations are impossible — i am hopelessly ugly, hopelessly silly

masturbation is impossible — my penis shrivels at my own touch

and i lack the most minimal powers of poetic imagination
necessary to conjure autoerotic fantasies

my gastrointestinal tract is listed as a must-to-avoid in the miche-
lin guide for intestinal parasites

wherever i am at the moment is the remotest frontier of the
diaspora

six flags, each depicting a still-frame from the zapruder film, flut-
ter above dealey plaza

and diffracted shards of sunlight impale the ornamental carp who
cough little bubbles of blood which cluster above the pond's
mosaic floor whose tiles of azure and crimson depict an
exploding head of ideas

as nearby, at james dean memorial hospital, nurses use cold bot-
tles of milk to cool the perspiring brows of surgeons who are
engraving ideas into the smooth tabula rasa brains of fetuses

an idea being that which exists at the moment a fly ball pauses at
the apex of its flight and bids the sky adieu . . .

that moment is pregnant

perhaps at that moment, in an s&m bar in plymouth, massachusetts, the 50-ft. woman staddles your face and defecates
17,000 scrabble letters, fertilizing the fallow fields of your
imagination . . .

and a new american style is born

when dawn came it was as if we'd been delivered stillborn from
an assemply line

identically curled in our bed

our arms crooked in perfect symmetry beneath our pillows

we were like twin fossils

two tipsy vertebrates who had crawled into a tar pool in the wee
hours of the pleistocene and slept through the tumult of
history

in our mouths the rich creamy taste and texture of raw sea
urchins, our breath was rank and aquatic

i pushed the hair from her forehead and her face was taut and
limned in shadow like a death mask

when the forensic pathologists performed their autopsy on you
they cried, those hardened professionals,
because peeling the skin from your head
was like peeling the skin from an onion

the flesh between your breasts
was a thin and pasty dough
which yielded easily to their scalpels

and the forensic pathologists, those hardened professionals,
shook their fists at the photographs of the 10 most wanted men,
one of whom murdered you, and wept

oh amy, what threnody matters
in a world whose software
enables a crossword puzzle, orphaned by your death,
to ask, "who now will do me?"

i am not roller-skating through piles of brittle autumn leaves
i am roller-skating down the aisles at macy's in narcotic slow
    motion to the music of john philip sousa
i'm skating past every surveillance camera
i'm skating across every closed-circuit television screen
salesmen come and go, murmuring, "jerry lewis est mort...jerry
    lewis est mort"
if only i had the software to conjure one macy's salesgirl at the
    end of this endless corridor into whose arms i'd roller-skate
    deliriously to the optimistic cornets of john philip sousa
but i don't have the appropriate software
and it would be brainless to continue skating

21

This piece is haunted like an old house. It sat two blocks from my parents' place, bike-riding distance. The sun rose in the sky like the flaw in my fingernail arcs toward the day I will bite it off. This piece limps toward the world with one part missing, and, in its place, the phantom pain of a boy's stance in my life.

Its central figurine can't get his due. Joe got bored, flew out the front door, is referential material built from the scraps he left lying around. For instance, I have a faded tuxedo ad we posed for. It was the late sixties. We were supposed to be "hippies" glaring suspiciously at "bourgeoisie" in our midst.

A blue light suffused the sky. The grass was painted green. The world is faked, head to toe. That's my dad's necktie restraining my long hair. I smirked when told to pass judgement on lives which dwarfed ours for the moment. "God" is the adjective I like to use when describing Joe, as it implies beliefs lost in the years since.

This piece has more in common with a tuxedo's luxurious order than our conspiratorial glances. Shyness invented our faces. Fear culls the words I write. Joe's beauty veiled the real world. Our lack of savoir faire ruined that ad. This world appreciates its faker aspects. Back then no one believed in us.

The ad was a monument to itself. We were just chipped, toppled statues, compliments to a gray suit which that civilization raised to a concept we'd written off. We were extremely pretentious to think we could represent more than our drugged selves. I like to praise things that don't deserve it.

No matter how I position it, that time's a threat. It stirs in its throne room of phony light like a young boy who's constructed a doll house around himself. If I could finish it I'd hide behind all this artifice and stab him hundreds of times, which is what I've been doing here, but I'd replace this blue pen with a knife, this page with juicier flesh.

The photographers left. It was just Joe and me and the afternoon. We would have lasted five minutes stretched out like that. Boredom, I mean. "Haunted house," I thought, motioning toward our bikes. Ten minutes later we snuck through its rusty and vine-draped gate. Its crisp front yard was a mess, the mansion shaggy with flakes of pre-weatherproof paint, from its peaked roof to the lopsided front porch. I pushed what was left of the door open. Joe trailed me in. His back, ass and legs became part of the inner dark. I'd picture them and lose my train of thought.

Maybe if Joe were here the whole issue of art would seem pointless beside him. I close my eyes and imagine he's lying face down. My hard-on enters his ass; my knife repeatedly stabs his back. His life is upped in its preciousness. I can continue to work.

We climbed the dangerous stairs, checking each room. Someone had scrawled "Fuck the pigs" in toy blood on one wall. Joe wore his "Timothy Leary for President" t-shirt. Blue letters, white cloth. His mood turned ugly at one point. He threw a can of dry paint through a pane of glass for kicks.

What did Joe want out of life? Something that only a head dull of drugs could suggest. Stringy brown hair, pinpricks for eyes, but I lusted after him no matter how many days in a row he had worn those pants. It's him I loved, not the idea of love, nor the effect of the joints we smoked, nor the descriptive abilities I've picked up since.

We crouched in what used to be someone's room. Remove the concept of ghosts, bulldoze the sketchy set, eliminate gothic overtones and what's left: two seeming nobodies fumbling for things to say.

"Let's try the roof."

"If you're sure we won't fall off."

I was Joe's beau, big brother, dad figure. That house is our love distilled into one spooky scene, where truth and wishes commingle. His sense of me was a little of both. My sense of him is complete fabrication. How could I know what went on in his head? Not by watching the back of his pants precede me up those steps.

The roof was falling apart. Loose shingles broke off and clacked to the ground as we strode across. It seemed the perfect spot to stretch out, light up. I wanted to fuck him right there and then. The danger implicit in our surroundings made compositional sense. I saw the big picture before I knew what was under my nose and behind Joe's illustrious face.

He was obscured by the smoke from a flickering joint. Instead of Joe, I saw a yellowing ad for the boy I'd have held if I wasn't so stoned out. He and the smoke and the skyline of trees seemed unnaturally poised, so my eyes took a photograph. Ours was a vague, high-gloss world with unsuitable tension inside it.

I can remember when, many years subsequent, traveling in Europe turned into a chore: flus piling up, tiffs with my traveling companions. I walked by myself to the tip of a jetty in Nice and stared out at the Mediterranean. Its turquoise depths were incredibly turbulent. I was "at peace" for the first time in decades.

Looking in Joe's eyes felt like that, the actual turbulence "lost" in their overall blueness. I thought, "Just go ahead and fall right into them. He's stoned and won't know the difference." We kissed for a while and then drew slightly apart, watching my hard-on deflate. I felt like tossing him down on the roof.

He felt: (1) peace. (2) afraid that refusing me would test our friendship. (3) guilty. (4) disappointment at what he perceived as my hidden intentions. (5) used. (6) drugged. (7) ?

Now, even more than then, I want to know. Once I imagined an autopsy in which Joe's feelings were pried open, figured out, placed in a poetic light. They're in a short story I'll never publish. But love's not like that. It eludes words, which are all I know how to create. It throws an old can of paint through a thin, polished work of art, then dashes off.

I rest my hand on my chest. Joe is still in here somewhere

throwing things around. He grabs a handful of words and breaks the hearts of those trying to get a good look at him. I say his name in a low, dispirited voice to no one in particular. I sound like a foreigner, don't I man?

Joe is alive in the work of an artist obsessed with him, trapped in a cave-in somewhere in these long-winded sentences. I could abandon him, then live my life with a tiny prickly voice in my head. Nothing a few drugs won't tone down. Or I can push all that's left of its door open and throw some light on that rickety house, or whatever remains of it.

All that remains is this cold, black rectangle of words I've been picking at. My eyes are peeled, but I can't see a thing for the dimness of what felt more bone-chilling back when I scaled its heights. Now I will lift my blue pen off this darkened page and check its structure for highlights, with chin in hand. A haunted piece in place of the love I would dream of from here on in.

———————————————

Malcolm Bennett and Aidan Hughes live in London.

Richard Brautigan was born in 1935 in the Pacific Northwest of
the United States. During his lifetime he published ten novels,
including *Trout Fishing in America, A Confederate General from
Big Sur* and *So The Wind Won't Blow It All Away*; nine volumes of
poetry, including *Please Plant This Book* and *The Pill Versus The
Springhill Mining Disaster*; and *Revenge of the Lawn*, a collection
of short fiction. He was a central figure of San Francisco's Haight-
Ashbury District during its heyday in the late 60s and early 70s,
and spent his later years in Tokyo and on a ranch in Montana. He
took his own life in 1984.

Raised in Rome, Italy, Anne Calcagno earned her B.A. from Williams College and her M.F.A. from the University of Montana. Her
stories have been accepted for publication in *The North American
Review, TriQuarterly, Denver Quarterly, Lake Effect, Fiction
Monthly, The Slackwater Review, Intro,* and *Epoch.* Her work
appears in two anthologies, *Fiction of the Eighties* (TriQuarterly
Books, 1990) and *American Fiction* (Birch Lane Press, 4th edition,
1991). In 1989 she received a National Endowment for the Arts
Creative Writing Fellowship for stories from her short story col-
lection *Married You Are Not Alone.* She teaches at the School of the
Art Institute of Chicago, and is currently at work on a novel.

Dennis Cooper is the author of several volumes of fiction and poetry, one of which, *The Tenderness of the Wolves*, was nominated for the Los Angeles Times Book Award for Poetry in 1984. He is the author of *Closer*, which won the 1990 Ferro-Grumley Award for Gay Fiction; *Frisk*, a novel which was published in 1991 by Grove Press; and *Wrong*, a collection of his short fictions which will be published by Grove Press in 1992. He has written a number of pieces for the stage, many of which were produced in collaboration with choreographer Ishmael Houston Jones. He lives in Los Angeles.

Nancy Davidson is an artist and writer. She was born in Chicago and received her M.F.A. from the Art Institute of Chicago. Presently she lives and works in New York City. Her work connects aspects of sexuality, gender, and memory. She uses the textual practice of feminism to exploit contradictions. Focusing on fact and fabrication, she criticizes patriarchy from within.

Richard Hawkins is an artist and writer living in Los Angeles. He received an M.F.A. in 1988 from the California Institute of the Arts. His visual work has been shown in New York, Los Angeles, and San Francisco, and his writings can be found in *Brains, Farm,* and *Dear World*. In 1991 he was included in *Discontent*, an anthology of new gay and lesbian fiction edited by Dennis Cooper, and participated as a panelist in the "Outwrite Gay and Lesbian Writer's Conference" in San Francisco.

Patricia Highsmith was born in Texas in 1931 and attended New York University in New York City. She has published more than twenty novels throughout her career, including *Strangers On A Train, Found In The Street, Tales of Natural and Unnatural Catastrophes, The Talented Mr. Ripley, Ripley Under Ground,* and *Ripley's Game*. Her five short story collections include *The Animal Lover's Book of Beastly Murder, The Black House,* and *Little Tales of Misogyny*. She lives and works in Zurich, Switzerland.

Richard House is a member of the Chicago-based collaborative,

Haha. His short fiction has been published in *Farm, Farm Boys, The Gentlewomen of California, The Village Voice Literary Supplement,* and *Whitewalls.*

Mark Leyner lives and works in Hoboken, New Jersey, with his wife, the psychotherapist Arleen Portada. He was born in Jersey City, New Jersey, in 1956, and graduated from Brandeis in 1977. His books include *I Smell Esther Williams*, published by Fiction Collective in 1983, and *My Cousin, My Gastroenterologist*, published in 1990 by Harmony/Crown Books. He is currently working on *Steroids Made My Friend Jorge Kill His Speech Therapist: An ABC After School Special*, to be published by Harmony/Crown in 1992.

Clarice Lispector was born in 1925 in the Ukraine. At that time, her parents were in the process of emigrating to Brazil, where they moved when she was two months old. After earning a law degree in 1944, she travelled throughout Switzerland, Italy, and the United States with her husband Mauri Gurgel Valente, who worked for the foreign service. They had two children during that time, and were divorced after they returned to Brazil in 1959. Her novels include *The Passion According to G. H., An Apprenticeship or The Book of Delights*, and *The Apple in the Dark*; her collections of short stories include *Family Ties* and *Soulstorm.* She died in Rio de Janeiro of cancer in 1977.

Patrick McGrath lives and works in New York City. His books include a collection of short stories titled *Blood and Water and Other Tales, The Grotesque*, a novel, and *Spider*, his most recent novel.

Virgilio Piñera was born in 1912 in Cardenas, Cuba. He studied literature and philosophy at Havana University, collaborating with the group that edited the review *Origenes*. Poverty and rebelliousness drove him to Argentina in 1950, where his first published short stories and novels earned the admiration of Jorge Luis Borges and Jose Bianco. In 1957 he returned to Cuba and worked for the daily newspaper *Revolucion*, but was arrested in 1961 for "political and moral crimes" — apparently for his refusal to write "socialist" literature and his overt homosexuality. His works include the novels *La Carne de Rene* and *Pequenas Maniobras*, the poetry collections *Las Furias* and *La Vida Entera*, and *Cuentos Frios*, a collection of short stories. He died in Havana in 1979. *Rene's Flesh*, an English translation of Piñera's first novel, was published by the Eridanos Press in 1990.

Anne Rice was born in New Orleans, where she now lives and works with her husband, the poet Stan Rice, and their son, Christopher. Her novels include *The Feast of All Saints, Interview With The Vampire, The Vampire Lestat*, and *Queen of the Damned*. She is currently at work on a new novel.

David Sedaris is a writer and performer currently living in New York City. His stories have appeared in *New American Writing, ACM, Dear World, The Los Angeles Journal of Contemporary Art, Farm, The Gentlewomen of California, Out/Look*, and *Whitewalls*. He was recently writing a play that was scheduled to open in New York's Theatre for The New City in September of 1991.

Victoria Tokareva lives in Moscow and has recently completed a collection of stories.

David Wojnarowicz lives and works in New York City. His artworks were included in the 1991 Biennial of the Whitney Museum of American Art, New York, and his book *CLOSE TO THE KNIVES; A Memoir of Disintegration*, was released by Random House in 1991.

M. W. Burns

born: 1958, Stamford, Connecticut
lives and works in Chicago

Education
1990 M.F.A., The School of the Art Institute of Chicago
1982 B.F.A., The University of the Arts, Philadelphia

Selected group exhibitions
1991 Northern Illinois University Gallery, Chicago,
"Articulations part 3," audio-text installation
1990 N.A.M.E. Gallery, Chicago, "Synapse," audio-text
installation
Detail in the Cottage: Re-Questing the Parlor, Randolph
Street Gallery, Chicago
1989 C.A.G.E., Cincinnati, "Collision," audio-text installation
1988 Nexus Contemporary Art Center, Atlanta, "Use only as
directed," audio-text installation
10 x 12, Fleisher Art Memorial, Philadelphia
Momenta Gallery, Philadelphia

Selected bibliography
Budd, Hildreth Ann. "Review, Nexus Contemporary Art Center,"
Art Papers, (Sept./Oct., 1988)
Morgan, Michele. "A Consonant Vowel," album review, *Dialogue,
An Art Journal*, (Mar./Apr. 1989)
_____. "Review, C.A.G.E. Cincinnati," *New Art Examiner*,
(June 1989)
Stevens, Mitchell. "Detail in the Cottage: Re-Questing the Parlor,"
New Art Examiner, (May, 1990)
Wainwright, Lisa. "Beyond Imagism," *Art International*,
(Summer, 1990)

Orshi Drozdik

born: 1947 in Budapest, Hungary
lives and works in New York

Education

1977   B.F.A., M.F.A., Budapest Fine Art Academy, Hungary

One-person exhibitions

1991   Gemeentemuseum, Arnhem
1990   *Fragmenta Naturae*, Tom Cugliani Gallery, New York
        Ernst Museum, Budapest
        Galerie Hans Knoll, Vienna
        Richard Anderson Gallery, New York
1989   *Morbid Conditions*, Tom Cugliani Gallery, New York
        ARCH, Amsterdam
1988   *Natural Philosophy*, Tom Cugliani Gallery, New York
        CEPA Gallery, Buffalo
1985   *Biological Metaphors*, Galerie Suspect, Amsterdam
        (travelled to Mercer Union, Toronto, and Budapest
        Galeria, Budapest)

Selected group exhibitions

1991   Galerie Air, Amsterdam
        Galerie Hans Knoll, Budapest
        Anni Novanta, Bologna
1990   Grazer Kunstverein, Graz, Austria
        About Nature: A Romantic Impulse, Barbara Toll Fine Arts,
        New York
        Memory-Reality, Ceres Gallery, New York
        Stendahl Syndrome: The Cure, Andrea Rosen Gallery,
        New York
        Natural History Recreated, The Center of Photography at
        Woodstock, Woodstock, New York
        Vanitas: The Collector's Cabinet, Curt Marcus Gallery,
        New York
1989   *Science/Technology/Abstraction: Art at the End of The
        Decade*, University Art Galleries, Wright State University,

Dayton, Ohio

Alternative Museum, New York

Strange Attractors: The Signs of Chaos, The New Museum
of Contemporary Art, New York

Art About AIDS, Freedman Gallery, Albright College,
Reading, Pennsylvania

Tierra Encantada, Kansas City Art Institute, Kansas City,
Missouri

A Good Read: The Book as Metaphor, Barbara Toll Fine
Arts, New York

1988   Doug Milford Gallery, New York

Tom Cugliani Gallery, New York

1987   *Metaphysics*, Piezo Electric, New York

1986   Stedelijk Museum, U.M.A., Amsterdam

Dystopia, Salon de Facto, New York

1985   Printed Matter, COLAB, New York

1984   *Eastern Europe*, El Bohio, New York

Jack Tilton, COLAB, New York

Selected bibliography

Adams, Brooks. "Grotesque Photography," *The Print Collector's
Newsletter*, (Jan./Feb. 1991)

Bruyn de, Eric. "Orshi Drozdik," *Forum*, (Jan./Feb., 1990)

Gookin, Kirby. "Review," *Artforum*, (May, 1989)

Haus, Mary Ellen. "Orshi Drozdik," Tom Cugliani Gallery,
Tema Celeste, (Apr./May, 1989)

Hayt-Akins, Elizabeth. "Envisioning the Yesterday of Tomorrow
and the Tomorrow of Today," *Contemporanea*, (Jan., 1991)

Heartney, Eleanor. "Review," *Art in America*, (June 1988)

_____. "Strong Debuts," *Contemporanea*, (July/Aug., 1988)

Indiana, Gary. "Science Holiday," *The Village Voice*,
(Mar. 15, 1988)

Levy Ellen. "Natural History Re-Created," *Center Quarterly*,
(vol. 11, no. 4, 1990)

Niesluchowski, W.G.J. "Orshi Drozdik: Adventures in Technos
Dystopium: Popular Natural Philosophy," *CEPA Journal*,
(vol. 4, no. 1, 1989)

Russell, John. "A Good Read: The Book as Metaphor: Barbara Toll
    Gallery," *New York Times*, (June 16, 1989)
Smith, Roberta. "An Array of Artists, Styles and Trends in
    Downtown Galleries," *New York Times*, (Feb., 1988)
Spector, Nancy. "Review," *Artscribe*, (Summer, 1989)
Veelen van, Ijsbrand. "Kunstzinnigdoktertje Spelen,"
    Het Parol, (Oct. 25, 1989)
Wei, Lilly. "The Peripatetic Artist: 14 Statements,"
    Art in America, (July, 1989)

Felix Gonzalez-Torres

born: 1957 in Guaimaro, Cuba
lives and works in New York

Education

1987   M.F.A., International Center for Photography,
       New York University
1983   Whitney Museum Independent Study Program
1983   B.F.A., Pratt Institute of Art, Brooklyn
1981   Whitney Museum Independent Study Program

One-person exhibitions

1991   *Every Week There is Something Different*, Andrea Rosen
       Gallery, New York
       Museum Fridericianum, Kassel, Germany
1990   Neue Gesellschaft fur Bildende Kunst, Berlin
       University of British Columbia, Vancouver, Canada
       Andrea Rosen Gallery, New York
1989   The Brooklyn Museum of Art, New York
1988   The Workspace, The New Museum of Contemporary Art,
       New York
       INTAR Gallery, New York
       Rastovski Gallery, New York

Selected group exhibitions

1991   *Biennial*, The Whitney Museum of American Art,

New York

From Desire: A Queer Diary, Richard Brush Gallery,
St. Lawrence University, New York

Something Pithier and More Psychological,
Simon Watson Gallery, New York

Felix Gonzalez-Torres and Michael Jenkins, Xavier
Hufkens Gallery, Brussels

The Savage Garden, Fundacion Caja de Pensiones, Madrid

1990   *The Rhetorical Image*, The New Museum of Contemporary
Art, New York

Stendahl Syndrome: The Cure, Andrea Rosen Gallery,
New York

Loving Correspondence, Massimo Audiello Gallery,
New York

Artedomani, Musei di Spoleto, Spoleto, Italy

Constructive Anger, Barbara Krakow Gallery, Boston

Collaborations, Andrea Rosen Gallery, New York

get well soon, Robbin Lockett Gallery, Chicago

Red, Galerie Christine & Isy Brachot, Brussels

This Symphony Shall Always Remain Untitled,
Terrain Gallery, San Francisco

Neue Gesellschaft fur Bildende Kunst, Berlin

The Clinic, Simon Watson Gallery, New York

New Langton Arts, San Francisco

Information, Terrain Gallery, San Francisco

1989   *New Acquisitions*, The Museum of Modern Art, New York

Art About AIDS, Freedman Gallery, Albright College,
Reading, Pennsylvania

Amerikarma, Hallwalls, Buffalo, New York

Double Take, Contemporary Arts Center, Cincinnati

To Probe and To Push: Artists of Provocation,
Wessell-O'Conner Gallery, New York

In the Center of Doubt, Massimo Audiello Gallery,
New York

After the Goldrush, Milford Gallery, New York

Matter/Anti-Matter, Terrain Gallery, San Francisco

1988   *Real World*, White Columns, New York

The Text is Not Explained, Stux Gallery, New York
Inserts, (advertising supplement inserted into the
Sunday *New York Times*), Group Material, New York
Corporate Crimes, Installations, San Diego

1987   *Selections*, Artist's Space, New York
The Castle, Group Material, Documenta VIII, Kassel,
Germany
The Fairy Tale, Artist's Space, New York

Selected bibliography

Atkins, Robert. "New This Week," *Seven Days*, (Feb. 21, 1990)
_____. "Art=Life," *Seven Days*, (May 24, 1989)
Avgikos, Jan. "This is My Body: Felix Gonzalez-Torres," *Artforum*,
    (Feb. 1991)
_____. "Nurse . . . The Screens!!," *Artscribe*, (Nov./Dec., 1990)
Barckert, Lynda. "New Humanism, *Reader* (Chicago),
    (May 25, 1990)
Brenson, Michael. "Felix Gonzalez-Torres," *New York Times*,
    (July 28, 1989)
Cameron, Dan. "The Look of Love," *Shift*, (vol. 3, 1989)
Chiodi, Stefano. "Review," *Contemporanea*, (Nov., 1990)
Chua, Lawrence. "Review," *Flash Art*, (Jan./Feb., 1990)
Cyphers, Peggy. "New York in Review," *Arts*, (Apr., 1990)
Decter, Joshua. "Review," *Arts*, (Mar., 1991)
Deitcher, David. "How Do You Memorialize a Movement
    That Isn't Dead?," *Village Voice*, (June 27, 1989)
Faust, Gretchen. "Review," *Arts*, (Jan., 1991)
Heartney, Eleanor. "Review," *Art in America*, (May, 1990)
Hess, Elizabeth. "New York to Helms: Drop Dead," *Village Voice*,
    (Oct. 24, 1989)
Indiana, Gary. "Vile Days," *Village Voice*, (June 28, 1989)
Kalin, Tom. "Prodigal Stories," *Aperture*, (Fall, 1990)
Levin, Kim. "Choices," *Village Voice*, (Jan. 8, 1991)
_____. "Art That Intervenes," *Village Voice*, (Jan. 15, 1991)
Liu, Catherine. "Review," *Flash Art*, (Oct., 1988)
Mahoney, Robert. "Review," *Flash Art*, (May/June, 1990)
McCoy, Pat. "Review," *Tema Celeste*, (Apr./June, 1990)

Pincus, Robert L. "Is Installation Exhibit the end-of-an-age Art?," *San Diego Union*, (Nov. 22, 1987)

Smith, Roberta. "The Group Show as Crystal Ball," *New York Times*, (July 6, 1990)

_____. "Minimalism On the March: More and More, Less and Less," *New York Times*, (Jan. 26, 1990)

Spector, Nancy. "Felix Gonzalez-Torres, *Contemporanea*, (Summer, 1989)

Spector, Nancy and Steven Evans. "Double Fear," *Parkett*, (no. 22, 1989)

Doug Hammett

born: 1963 in Alhambra, California
lives and works in Pasadena, California

Education
1989   M.F.A., Art Center School of Design, Pasadena
1985   B.F.A., University of Redlands, California

Selected group exhibitions
1989   *LOADED*, Richard Kuhlenschmidt Gallery, Santa Monica, California
        Against Nature, L.A.C.E., Los Angeles

Selected bibliography
Artweek. "After Modernism, After AIDS, Against Nature," (Feb. 4, 1989)

Breslauer, Jan. "Nature Morte," *L.A. Weekly*, (Jan. 20, 1989)

Fehlau, Fred. "Who's Nature," *Art Issues*, (May, 1989)

Kandel, Susan. "Review," *Arts*, (Nov., 1989)

Knight, Christopher. "Transforming our view of the AIDS experience," *Los Angeles Herald Examiner*, (Jan. 15, 1989)

Wendy Jacob

born: 1958 in Rochester, New York
lives and works in Chicago

Education
1989   M.F.A., The School of the Art Institute of Chicago
1980   B.A., Williams College, Williamstown, Massachusetts
1976   Mount Holyoke College, South Hadley, Massachusetts

One-person exhibitions
1990   Andrea Rosen Gallery, New York (with Zoe Leonard)
1988   *Spiro*, Goodrich Gallery, Williams College, Williamstown,
        Massachusetts

Selected group exhibitions
1991   *Biennial*, The Whitney Museum of American Art,
        New York
        Breathing Room, Amy Lipton Gallery, New York
        Esther Schipper Gallery, Cologne, Germany
        Galerie Walcheturm, Zurich
1990   *get well soon*, Robbin Lockett Gallery, Chicago
        Plenty, Kansas City Art Institute, Missouri,
        (installation by the collaborative group Haha: Richard
        House, Wendy Jacob, Laurie Palmer, John Ploof)
        Murmur, LaFollette Park, Chicago (Haha collaborative
        installation)
1989   *Biokinetic*, University Galleries, Illinois State University,
        Normal (travelled to Western Gallery, Western
        Washington University, Bellingham, Washington)
        Our Corner of the World, University Galleries, Illinois
        State University, Normal
        Plus, Robbin Lockett Gallery, Chicago

Selected bibliography
Artpark. *1987 Visual Arts Program*, catalogue, essay by Judd
    Tully. Lewiston, New York: 1987.
Barckert, Lynda. "New Humanism," *Reader* (Chicago), (May 25,
    1990)

Doyle, Maggie. "Haha Installation 'Housekeeping',"
    P-form, (February, 1989)

Gamble, Allison. "The Myths that Work," *New Art Examiner*,
    (May, 1989)

Golden, Deven. "'Murmur' Raises a Din," *New Art Examiner*,
    (June, 1990)

Illinois State University. *Our Corner of The World: Seventeen
    Illinois Artists*, exhibition catalogue, essay by Laurie
    Dahlberg. Normal, Illinois: 1989.

_____. *Biokinetic*, exhibition catalogue, "Biokinetic: Poetry
    Through Motion" essay by Peter Spooner. Normal, Illinois:
    1989.

Schwabsky, Barry. "Wendy Jacob/Zoe Leonard," *Arts*,
    (October, 1990)

Schwartzman, Alan. "Art: Group Show." *New Yorker*,
    (June, 1990)

Liz Larner

born: 1960 in Sacramento, California
lives and works in Los Angeles

Education
1985   B.F.A., California Institute of the Arts, Valencia

One-person exhibitions
1991   Stuart Regan Gallery, Los Angeles
1990   303 Gallery, New York
        Galleri Nordanstad-Skarstedt, Stockholm
1989   303 Gallery, New York
        Galerie Peter Pakesch, Vienna
1988   Margo Leavin Gallery, Los Angeles

Selected group exhibitions
1991   *New Work by Gallery Artists*, 303 Gallery, New York
1990   *Drawings*, Luhring/Augustine/Hetzler, Santa Monica,
        California

The Köln Show, Cologne, Germany

Liz Larner, Rosemarie Trockel, Meg Webster, Stuart Regan
Gallery, Los Angeles

Luhring Augustine, New York

nonrePRESENTation, Security Pacific Corporation
Gallery, Los Angeles

Signs of Life: Process and Materials, 1960–1990,
Institute of Contemporary Art, University of Pennsylvania,
Philadelphia

Artificial Nature, Deste Art Foundation for Contemporary
Art, The House of Cyprus, Athens

Stendahl Syndrome: The Cure, Andrea Rosen Gallery,
New York

Mind Over Matter, The Whitney Museum of American Art,
New York

Galerie Sophia Ungers, Cologne, Germany

1989   *Biennial*, The Whitney Museum of American Art,
New York

The Desire of the Museum, The Whitney Museum of
American Art, Downtown at the Federal Plaza, New York

Galerie Ryszard Varisella, Frankfurt, Germany

David Cabrera, Larry Johnson, Liz Larner, 303 Gallery,
New York

Archeology II, Roy Boyd Gallery, Los Angeles

Specific Metaphysics, Sandra Gering Gallery, New York

1988   303 Gallery, New York

Re:Placement, L.A.C.E., Los Angeles

A Drawing Show, Cable Gallery, New York

Life Like, Lorence Monk Gallery, New York

Graz, Stadtmuseum, Graz, Austria

Dennis Anderson Gallery, Los Angeles

1987   *Room 9*, Tropicana Hotel, West Hollywood, California

Nothing Sacred, Margo Leavin Gallery, Los Angeles

1987 Annuale, L.A.C.E., Los Angeles

Jeffrey Lind Gallery, Los Angeles

Reworks: Recent Sculptures, New Langton Arts,
San Francisco

L.A. Hot and Cool, List Visual Art Center, Massachusetts Institute of Technology, Cambridge, Massachusetts

Selected bibliography

Andrea Rosen Gallery. *Stendhal Syndrome: The Cure*, exhibition catalogue, essays by Rhonda Lieberman, Catherine Liu and Laurence Rickels. Andrea Rosen Gallery, New York: 1990.

Avgikos, Jan. "Review," *Flash Art*, (Oct., 1990)

Bonetti, David. "Welcome to L.A.: Art that blows hot and cool," *The Boston Phoenix*, (Jan. 15, 1988)

Brenson, Michael. "In the Arena of the Mind, at the Whitney," *New York Times*, (Oct. 19, 1990)

Cameron, Dan. "Changing Priorities in American Art," *Art International*, (Spring, 1990)

Cotter, Holland. "Report from New York," *Art in America*, (Sept., 1989)

Decter, Joshua. "Review," *Artscribe*, (Sept./Oct., 1990)

Deste Art Foundation. *Artificial Nature,* exhibition catalogue, essay by Jeffrey Deitch. Deste Art Foundation for Contemporary Art, Athens, Greece: 1990.

Fehlau, Fred. "Review," *Flash Art*, (Dec., 1988)

Gardner, Colin. "Review," *Artforum*, (Jan., 1989)

Gerstler, Amy. "Review," *Art Issues*, (Jan., 1989)

Gookin, Kirby. "Review," *Artforum*, (Oct., 1990)

Grove, Nancy. "Angle of Vision: Tradition and Its Discontents," *Art & Antiques*, (Nov., 1990)

Indiana, Gary. "Science Holiday," *Village Voice*, (Mar. 15, 1988)

Institute of Contemporary Art. *Signs of Life: Process and Materials, 1960–1990*, exhibition catalogue, essay by Melissa E. Feldman. Institute of Contemporary Art, University of Pennsylvania, Philadelphia: 1990.

Jones, Amelia. "Museum Bashing," *Art International*, (Sept., 1988)

Kandel, Susan. "L.A. in Review," *Arts*, (May, 1990)

Kelley, Mike. "Foul Perfection: (Thoughts on Caricature)," *Artforum*, (Jan., 1989)

Knight, Christopher. "L.A. Lately," *Elle*, (Dec., 1989)

————. "Whitney Biennial review," *Los Angeles Herald*

Examiner, (May 7, 1989)

_____. "Re:Placement Parts," *Los Angeles Herald Examiner*,
    (Mar. 20, 1988)

Larson, Kay. "Every Object Tells a Story," *New York*,
    (Oct. 29, 1990)

_____. "The Children's Hour," *New York*, (Summer, 1989)

Miller, John. "Review," *Artscribe*, (Jan./Feb., 1989)

Morgan, Robert. "New York in Review," *Arts*, (Summer, 1989)

Pagel, David. "Review," *Arts*, (Dec., 1988)

Schjeldahl, Peter. "Theory-itis," *Seven Days*,
    (Aug. 23, 1989)

Security Pacific Corporation Gallery. *nonrePRESENTation*,
    exhibition catalogue, essay by Colin Gardner. Security
    Pacific Corporation Gallery, Los Angeles: 1990

Smith, Roberta. "The Whitney Interprets Museums' Dreams,"
    New York Times, (July 23, 1989)

_____. "Art That Hails from the Land of Deja Vu,"
    New York Times, (June 4, 1989)

_____. "More Women and Unknowns in the Whitney
    Biennial," *New York Times*, (Apr. 28, 1989)

Stals, Jose Lebrero. "The Köln Show," *Flash Art*,
    (Oct., 1990)

Taylor, Robert. "'L.A. Hot and Cool' a Rewarding Exhibit,"
    The Boston Globe, (Jan. 17, 1988)

von Kunstadt, Theodor. "Review," *Flash Art*,
    (Summer, 1989)

Yau, John. "Official Policy," *Arts*, (Sept., 1989)

Patty Martori

born: 1956 in Phoenix, Arizona
lives and works in New York

Education
1980   B.F.A., San Francisco Art Institute

1983   M.F.A., Yale University School of Art

One-person exhibitions

1990   Ryszard Varisella Pavilion, Frankfurt, Germany
        Pat Hearn Gallery, New York
1989   Pat Hearn Gallery, New York

Selected group exhibitions

1991   *Total Metal*, Simon Watson Gallery, New York
1990   *The Status of Sculpture*, Institute of Contemporary Art,
        London (travelled to the Musée St. Pierre, Lyon)
        Ralph Wernicke, Stuttgart
        The Köln Show, Cologne, Germany
1989   Galerie Varisella, Frankfurt, Germany
        Pat Hearn Gallery, New York
1988   *Snug Harbor Sculpture Festival*, Newhouse Center,
        Staten Island, New York

Selected bibliography

Corris, Michael. "The Status of Sculpture," ICA, London,
        Artscribe, (Jan./Feb., 1991)
Dector, Joshua. "Review," *Arts*, (May, 1989)
_____. "Review," *Artscribe*, (Summer, 1990)
_____. "Review," *Contemporanea*, (Oct., 1990)
Humphrey, David. "Review," *Art Issues*, (Feb., 1990)
Larson, Kay. "Review," *New York*, (Feb., 1989)
Stals, Jose L. "The Köln Show," *Flash Art*, (Oct., 1990)

Laurie Palmer

born: 1958 in Albany, New York
lives and works in Chicago

Education

1988   M.F.A., The School of the Art Institute of Chicago
1981   B.A., Williams College, Williamstown, Massachusetts

One-person exhibitions

1990   *Natural History*, Frontage Gallery, Santa Barbara, California

1989   *Winterflush: a Temporary Garden*, Artist's Space, New York

          Untitled Installation, Goodrich Gallery, Williams College, Williamstown, Massachusetts

Selected group exhibitions

1990   *Vanitas: The Collector's Cabinet*, Curt Marcus Gallery, New York

          The Mussel Secretes the Shell that Shapes It, N.A.M.E. Gallery, Chicago

          Conceptual Installations, Illinois State Museum, Springfield

          Murmur, LaFollette Park Fieldhouse, Chicago, (installation by the collaborative group Haha: Richard House, Wendy Jacob, Laurie Palmer, John Ploof)

1989   *Faculty exhibition*, University of California, Santa Barbara

          Panel Discussion from Chicago, Woodland Pattern Bookstore, Milwaukee

1988   *Detail in the Cottage*, Randolph Street Gallery, Chicago

          Housekeeping, Walkers Point Center for the Arts, Milwaukee, (Haha collaborative installation)

          New Faces, New Places, ARC Gallery, Chicago

          Open House, 857 North Winchester, Chicago, (Haha collaborative installation)

          Engaged Objects, N.A.M.E. Gallery, Chicago

1987   *Selections From The Permanent Collection*, The Museum of Contemporary Art, Chicago

          The White Show, MoMing Dance and Arts Center, Chicago

Selected bibliography

Bulka, Michael. "Review," *Dialogue*, (Nov., 1988)

Gamble, Allison. "Chicago: The Myths That Work," *New Art Examiner*, (May, 1989)

Golden, Deven. "Murmur Raises a Din," *New Art Examiner*, (June, 1990)

————. "Review," *New Art Examiner*, (Sept., 1988)

_____. "Review," *New Art Examiner*, (Mar., 1987)

Hixson, Kathryn. "Chicago in Review," *Arts*, (Apr., 1990)

Rosenbaum, Amy. "Review," *New Art Examiner*, (June, 1988)

Scanlan, Joseph. "Review," *Artscribe*, (May, 1990)

Sarah Seager

born: 1958 in Springfield, Massachussetts
lives and works in Pasadena, California

Education
1987   M.F.A., University of California, Los Angeles
1982   B.F.A., University of California, Berkeley

One-person exhibitions
1991   Burnett Miller Gallery, Los Angeles
1989   Dennis Anderson Gallery, Los Angeles

Selected group exhibitions
1991   Anselmo Alvarez, Madrid
1990   Galerie Schurr, Stuttgart, Germany
        Massimo Audiello, New York
        Contingent Realms: Four Contemporary Sculptors,
        The Whitney Museum of American Art at the Equitable
        Center, New York
        5th Anniversary Exhibition, Burnett Millery Gallery,
        Los Angeles
        Luhring / Augustine / Hetzler Gallery, Los Angeles
        Gallery Lelong, New York
1989   *LOADED*, Richard Kuhlenschmidt Gallery, Santa Monica,
        California
        Asher-Faure Gallery, Los Angeles
        Dennis Anderson Gallery, Los Angeles

Selected bibliography
Anderson, Michael. "Review," *Art in America*, (Dec., 1989)

Brenson, Michael. "Contingent Realms: Four Contemporary
    Sculptors," *New York Times*, (Oct. 19, 1990)

Curtis, Cathy. "The Galleries," *Los Angeles Times*, (Aug. 12, 1989)

Frank, Peter. "Art Pick of the Week," *L.A. Weekly*, (Sept. 1, 1989)

_____. "To be Young, Gifted and Los Angeleno," *Visions Magazine*, (Summer, 1989)

Hirsch, Jeffrey. "Work in Progress: A Portfolio of Emerging L.A. Artists," *L.A. Style*, (June 1990)

Knight, Christopher. "Group Art Shows Bloom in August," *Los Angeles Herald Examiner*, (Aug. 11, 1989)

_____. "L.A. Lately," *Elle*, (Dec., 1989)

_____. "Group Shows," *New Yorker*, (July 16, 1990)

Stevens, Richard. "Aspects of Our Corporeal Selves," *Artweek*, (Aug. 12, 1989)

David Sedaris

born: 1956 in Johnson City, New York
lives and works in New York

Education

1987   B.F.A., The School of the Art Institute of Chicago

1976   Kent State University, Kent, Ohio

1975   Western Carolina University, Cullowhee, North Carolina

One-person exhibitions

1983   *Decoy*, Southeastern Center for Contemporary Art, Winston-Salem, North Carolina

Selected group exhibitions

1990   *The Sinister: Sinister Art and the Art of The Sinister*, N.A.M.E. Gallery, Chicago

1989   *Panel Discussion from Chicago*, Woodland Pattern Bookstore, Milwaukee
        Encampments, Randolph Street Gallery, Chicago

1987   *With Words*, MoMing Dance and Art Center, Chicago

1984   *Masquerade*, Southeastern Center for Contemporary Art, Winston-Salem, North Carolina

1983   *Sculpture, First Juried Exhibition of North Carolina*

Crafts, North Carolina Museum of History, Raleigh

1982   *Sculpture, Wake County Artist's Exhibition*, North Carolina
State University, Raleigh
Nine from North Carolina, Sawtooth Center for
Visual Arts and the North Carolina Governor's School,
Winston-Salem

Selected readings

1990   *Diary Entries*, Chicagoland Public Radio 91.5 WBEZ,
Chicago

1989   *Origins of the Underclass*, Simon Watson Gallery,
New York

1988   *The Speckled Band*, Chicago Filmmakers, Chicago
The New Music, MoMing Dance and Art Center, Chicago
My Manuscript, Kathleen Edelman Gallery, Chicago

1987   *Public Notice*, Links Hall, Chicago
Jamboree, Limelight, Chicago
Diary Entries, Chicago Filmmakers, Chicago
Crafty, Marianne Deson Gallery, Chicago
Close To You, Randolph Street Gallery, Chicago
Candelabra, Limelight, Chicago

Plays produced

1989   *Walking Through Destiny's Plaything*, Link's Hall, Chicago

1987   *Life Imitates Archy*, Link's Hall, Chicago

1982   *Guilt by Association*, North Carolina Museum of Art,
Raleigh

Kiki Smith

born: 1954 in Nuremberg, Germany
lives and works in New York

Education
self-taught

One-person exhibitions

1991   Center for Contemporary Art, Amsterdam

University Art Museum, University of California, Berkeley

1990   *Projects: Kiki Smith*, The Museum of Modern Art,
New York

Centre d'Arte Contemporaine, Geneva

Fawbush Gallery, New York

The Clocktower, Institute for Art and Urban Resources,
New York

Tyler Gallery, Tyler School of Art, Philadelphia

1989   Galerie Rene Blouin, Montreal, Canada

Center for the Arts, Wesleyan University, Middletown,
Connecticut

Concentrations 20, The Dallas Museum of Art, Texas

1988   Fawbush Gallery, New York

1982   *Life Wants to Live*, The Kitchen, New York

Selected group exhibitions

1991   Simon Watson Gallery, New York

1990   Holly Solomon Gallery, New York

Recent Acquisitions, Corcoran Gallery of Art,
Washington, D.C.

Jack Tilton Gallery, New York

Figuring the Body, The Museum of Fine Arts, Boston

Group Material: AIDS Timeline, The Wadsworth Athe-
neum, Hartford, Connecticut

The Unique Print: 70s into 90s, The Museum of Fine Arts,
Boston

Fragments, Parts, and Wholes, White Columns, New York

Diagnosis, The Art Gallery of York University, Toronto

1990   *Witness Against Our Vanishing*, Artist's Space, New York

Stained Sheets/Holy Shrouds, Krieger-Landau Gallery,
Los Angeles

1989   *Projects and Portfolios*, The Brooklyn Museum of Art,
New York

Tom Cugliani Gallery, New York

Cara Perlman and Kiki Smith, Fawbush Gallery, New York

New York Experimental Glass, The Society for Art in Craft,
Pittsburgh

1988   *Desire Path*, Schulman Sculpture Garden, White Plains, New York

Committed To Print, The Museum of Modern Art, New York

A Choice, Kunstrai, Amsterdam

In Bloom, IBM Gallery, New York

Recent Acquisitions: 1986–1988, The Museum of Modern Art, New York

Arch Gallery, Amsterdam

1987   Fawbush Gallery, New York

Emotope, Buro-Berlin, Berlin

Kiki Smith: Drawings, Piezo Electric Gallery, New York

1986   *Donald Lipski, Matt Mullican and Kiki Smith*, The Clocktower, Institute for Art and Urban Resources, New York

Public and Private: American Prints Today, The Brooklyn Museum of Art, New York

Momento Mori, Centro Cultural Arte, Polanco, Mexico

1985   *Synaethics*, P.S. 1 Museum, Long Island City, New York

Male Sexuality, Art City, New York

Moderna Museet, Stockholm

1984   *Kiki Smith, Bill Taggert and Tod Wizon*, Jack Tilton Gallery, New York

1984: Women in New York, Galerie Engstrom, Stockholm

Inside/Out, Piezo Electric Gallery, New York

Modern Masks, The Whitney Museum of American Art, New York

360 Kunst-Speil, Wuppertal, Germany

1983   Hallwalls, Buffalo, New York

Science and Prophesy, White Columns, New York

Emergence: New Work from the Lower East Side, Susan Caldwell Gallery, New York

Island of Negative Utopia, The Kitchen, New York

1982   *Natural History*, Grace Borgenicht Gallery, New York

Fashion Moda Store, Documenta VII, Kassel, Germany

A More Store, Barbara Gladstone Gallery, New York

1981   *Cave Created Chaos*, White Columns, New York

TEUGUM COLAB, Geneva

Lightning, P.S. 1 Museum, Long Island City, New York

New York, New Wave, P.S. 1 Museum, Long Island City, New York

1980   *A More Store*, COLAB, New York

Manifesto Show, 5 Bleecker Street, New York

Time Square Show, New York

Selected bibliography

Adams, Brooks. "Review," *Art in America*, (Sept. 1988)

Brenson, Michael. "Review," (Donald Lipski, Matt Mullican and Kiki Smith at The Clocktower), *New York Times*, (Jan. 10, 1986)

The Brooklyn Museum of Art, *Projects and Portfolios: The 25th National Print Exhibition*, catalogue essay by T. Barry Walker. Brooklyn, New York: 1989.

Decter, Joshua. "Review," *Flash Art*, (Oct., 1989)

Faust, Wolfgang Max. "Emotope: A Project for Buro-Berlin," *Artforum*, (Jan., 1988)

Feitlowitz, Maugerite. "Where Art and Medicine Meet," *MD*, (Feb., 1984)

Hayt Atkins, Elizabeth. "Envisioning the Yesterday of Tomorrow and the Tomorrow of Today," *Contemporanea*, (Jan., 1991)

Levin, Kim. "Voice Picks" (Centerfold), *Village Voice* (June 21, 1988)

Lyons, Chris. "Kiki Smith: Body and Soul," *Artforum*, (Feb., 1990)

Mahoney, Robert. "Review," *Arts*, (Sept. 1988)

Mays, John Bentley. "Exploring The Human Body," *The Globe and Mail* (Toronto), (Jan. 19, 1990)

McCormick, Carlo. "Review," *Artforum*, (Oct., 1988)

Princenthal, Nancy. "Review," *Artnews*, (Apr., 1984)

Raynor, Vivian. "Review," *New York Times*, (May 11, 1984)

Robinson, Walter, and Carlo McCormick. "Slouching Toward Avenue D," *Art in America*, (Summer, 1984)

Schwendenwein, Jude. "Mysteries of the Body Re-Created," *The Hartford Courant* (Connecticut), (June 11, 1989)

Skoggard, Ross. "Review," *Art in America*, (Jan., 1982)

Smith, Roberta. "Review," *New York Times*, (Nov. 23, 1990)

_____. "Review," *New York Times*, (June 1, 1990)

_____. "Review," *New York Times*, (June 24, 1988)

The Society for the Arts in Crafts, *New York Experimental Glass* exhibition catalogue, essay by Karen Chambers. Pittsburgh, Pennsylvania: 1989

Tallman, Susan. "The Other Biennial," *Arts*, (Feb., 1990)

Tatransky, Valentin. "Review," *Arts*, (Jan., 1982)

Wagemans, Fred. "Fortunately and Happily Conditioned," *HP Magazine*, (May 21, 1988)

Waite, John. "Kiki Smith Pro Vita," *Metropolism*, (no. 5, 1985)

Wells, Jennifer. "The Body as a Democracy," *MOMA Members Quarterly*, (Fall 1990)

Wesleyan University, Center for the Arts, *Kiki Smith*, exhibition catalogue, essay by Klaus Ottman. Middletown, Connecticut: 1989

Sean Smith

born: 1960 in Waldwick, New Jersey
lives and works in Pasadena, California

Education
1988   B.F.A., California Institute of the Arts, Valencia, California
1986   A.D., University of Texas, Dallas

Selected group exhibitions
1986   *Biannually*, Nexus Contemporary Art Center, Atlanta, Georgia

M. W. Burns

Untitled, 1991
Wood, drywall, paint
11 x 6 x 5 feet
Lent by the artist

Articulations, Part I, 1989/90
Audio-text installation
Public address speakers, audio
equipment
Lent by the artist

Articulations, Part II, 1990
Audio-text installation
Public address speakers, audio
equipment
Lent by the artist

Orshi Drozdik

Erythrocyte, 1988
Porcelain, sandblasted glass, lead,
wood
7½ x 72 x 216 inches
Lent by the artist, courtesy of
Tom Cugliani Gallery, New York

Orshi Drozdik	*Lues Venerea*, 1988
	Springs, silk, glass jars, lead, steel, glass
	36¾ x 30½ x 13¾ inches
	Lent by the artist, courtesy of
	Tom Cugliani Gallery, New York
	Ether Anaesthesia, 1988
	Metal, porcelain, plastic tubing, lead, steel, glass
	34½ x 25 x 13½ inches
	Lent by the artist, courtesy of
	Tom Cugliani Gallery, New York
	My Mother's Medicine Cabinet, 1990
	Glass case with pharmaceuticals
	34½ x 25 x 13¾ inches
	Lent by the artist, courtesy of
	Tom Cugliani Gallery, New York
Felix Gonzalez-Torres	*Untitled (Loverboy)*, 1990
	Paper, endless copies
	7½ x 29 inches
	Lent by the Andrea Rosen collection, New York
	Untitled (t-cell count), 1990
	Graphite, colored pencil, gouache on paper, wood frame
	19½ x 15¾ inches
	Lent by the artist, courtesy of
	Andrea Rosen Gallery, New York

Doug Hammett

Untitled, 1989
Sizzling Red lipstick, gift box
10 x 9 inches
Lent by the artist

Untitled, 1991
Vanilla frosting, wood
48 x 3 x 3 inches
Lent by the artist

Untitled, 1991
Chocolate fudge frosting, wood
48 x 3 x 3 inches
Lent by the artist

Sleeping Beauty, 1988
HIV-positive blood, acrylic resin,
wood, sand
10 x 9 x 10 inches
Lent by Peter Liashkov, Los Angeles

Wendy Jacob

Ceiling, 1991
Rubber, wood, vinyl, and motors
Lent by the artist, courtesy of
Robbin Lockett Gallery, Chicago

Liz Larner

The Desire of the Museum Cultures:
Timothy Landers, "Anti-Bodies"
(semen and blood); Jackie McAllister,
"Scotch Mist" (whisky and haggis);
Catsou Roberts, "Gynecology"
(semen); Benjamin Weil, "Museology"
(dust from the museum floor and
walls); Marek Wieczorek, "Melancho-
lia, Mania, Utopia" (three tears, a
hair, and a wish), 1989
Mixed media in nutrient agar, glass,
display case
Lent by the artist, courtesy of
303 Gallery, New York

Body Cultures (Somebody, Anybody,
Nobody, Everybody, Your Body) 1991
Nutrient agar, glass, food coloring,
stainless steel, aluminum
¾ x 3 x 8 inches
Lent by the artist, courtesy of
303 Gallery, New York

Patty Martori

Untitled, 1990
Human hair
10 x 420 x 7 inches
Lent by the artist, courtesy of
Pat Hearn Gallery, New York

Untitled, 1990
Wood, bed sheets, silver bells
10 x 160 x 13 inches
Lent by the artist, courtesy of
Pat Hearn Gallery, New York

Laurie Palmer

Scent, 1990
Blown glass, sweat smells, stitchery,
atomizer top
6 x 15 x 15 inches
Lent by the artist

Scent, 1990
Blown glass, sweat smells, stitchery,
atomizer top
6 x 15 x 15 inches
Lent by the artist

Scent, 1990
Blown glass, sweat smells, stitchery,
rabbit fur, atomizer top
6 x 15 x 15 inches
Lent by the artist

Scent, 1990
Blown glass, sweat smells, stitchery,
atomizer top
6 x 15 x 15 inches
Lent by the artist

Cold Frame, 1989
Wood, glass, peat moss, cooked
cabbages
40 x 43 x 12 inches
Lent by the artist

Cold Frame, 1989
(Installed outside, in the quadrangle,
adjacent to the Divinity School)
Wood, glass, peat moss, cooked
cabbages
40 x 43 x 12 inches
Lent by the artist

Sarah Seager

Untitled, 1989
Porcelain, enamel on steel, wooden
tool handles
42 x 24 inches
Lent by Daniel Moquay, Paradise
Valley, Arizona

A Record of 100,000 Sighs, 1989
Recorded sound on vinyl, latex,
Plexiglas, wood
30 x 144 x 18 inches
Lent by Jay Chiat Collection, Venice,
California

Song for the Participation of Letters,
1990
Fluorescent lights, electrical wire,
enamel sign paint
62 x 128 x 4 inches
Lent by the artist, courtesy of Luhring
Augustine Gallery, New York

David Sedaris

Mechanical Heart, 1991
Basswood, wind-up mechanism
8 x 9 x 9 inches
Lent by the artist

Mechanical Heart, 1991
Basswood, wind-up mechanism
6 x 4 x 4⅛ inches
Lent by the artist

David Sedaris	*Mechanical Heart*, 1991
	Pine, wind-up mechanism
	9 x 2⅞ x 2⅞ inches
	Lent by the artist
	Mechanical Heart, 1991
	Basswood, wind-up mechanism
	7 x 9 x 9 inches
	Lent by the artist
Kiki Smith	*Digestive System*, 1988
	Ductile iron
	62 x 26 inches
	Lent by Tom Otterness, New York
	Untitled, 1990
	Wax, wood, cheesecloth
	30 x 50 x 4 inches
	Lent by the artist, courtesy of
	Fawbush Gallery, New York
	Dowry Cloth, 1991
	Human hair, wool
	7½ x 28½ x 24 inches
	Lent by the artist, courtesy of
	Fawbush Gallery, New York
Sean Smith	*Penetration*, 1988
	Installation, various media
	10 x 20 x 15 feet
	Lent by the artist

This catalogue exists in conjunction with an exhibition at The Renaissance Society in the Spring of 1991. Given the multi-sensual, experiential, often personal or confrontational nature of this work, it seemed more appropriate to have the text of the catalogue be a similar and equal interaction with reproductions and texts, as opposed to a publication that documented or analyzed the exhibition in whatever auxiliary ways. Each of the twelve artists in *The Body*, then, were asked to suggest fiction writers to be published alongside reproductions of their work, in lieu of essays by art historians or critics. We were confident that the fiction writer each artist suggested would somehow relate to the overall content and spirit of their works, and by extension inform other artworks and stories in the catalogue as well.

Most artists suggested several stories by the same writer, some several writers; in such instances we worked toward those pieces which we felt were most relevant and most recent. Those stories and writers that initially seemed outside of our initial idea of the collection were ultimately retained in deference to the exhibiting artists.

Nonetheless, however fair this approach was with respect to the catalogue's visual artists we felt that certain *literary* gaps remained: women writers; a writer with a particularly futuristic or "cyberpunk" bent; a slow-moving, poetic, traditional piece of prose; and, quite simply, some humor and happiness.

There's humor here but it's mostly ironic and dark. The happiness that exists is resigned, recuperative, persevering at best, and comes only after certain trials have been borne. We became conscious of these and other aspects as the collection took shape, and now feel very strongly about the significance — and coincidence — of its overall outlook and tone.

Joseph Scanlan, Editor

Acknowledgments

The Body broadens The Renaissance Society's investigation of artistic concerns at the beginning of the 1990s. When added to our recent sculpture exhibition and video program, this fiction collection reflects very deep cross-cultural concerns. This publication is put forth to acknowledge the urgency of the shift from issues of the marketplace to personal desires for a reunification of mind and body.

Our deepest gratitude goes first to the artists and writers, for so generously sharing their resources, information, and above all their confidence, which we have enjoyed throughout this project. Not only have they made these programs possible, but also rewarding for all of us at The Society who have had the pleasure to work with them.

We are especially grateful to John Vinci, architect and friend, for his assistance with the installation design; to Michael Glass and Michael Glass Design of Chicago for the excellence and generosity in their design work on the book and exhibition invitation; to Paul Baker Typography for their careful work with the typesetting; to Jean Fulton for her careful proofreading; and to Eastern Press for their production expertise.

Special thanks are extended to the staff of The Renaissance Society: to Thomas K. Ladd, Development Director; to Joseph Scanlan, Assistant Director; to Karen Reimer, Preparator; to Patricia A.

Scott, bookkeeper and secretary; and to Paul Coffey, Steven Drake and Susan Nowicki, gallery assistants. Their personal interest and diligent work greatly strengthened the organization of the exhibition, video program, and this publication.

Above all we are appreciative of the cooperation received from the many lenders to the exhibition. They deserve special recognition for their support of the artists, and for their generosity in sharing their works with us.

As always, my deep appreciation and gratitude for their continuing support and trust go to the Board of Directors of The Renaissance Society. I hope the reader will take the time to look through the list of these outstanding individuals from the Chicago community who contribute so generously of their time, energy and resources.

The exhibition and publication has been funded in part by generous grants from The National Endowment for the Arts, a federal agency; the Illinois Arts Council, a state agency; the City Arts Program of the Chicago Department of Cultural Affairs; and by our Membership. Indirect support has been received from the Institute of Museum Services, a federal agency offering general operating support to the nation's museums. Generous support has also been received from the Lannan Foundation and from Board member Timothy Flood and his wife Suzette. The support of these agencies, foundations and individuals has been vital, and our gratitude is extended to them.

We have received a very important new grant this year from The Elizabeth Firestone Graham Foundation towards the publication of all catalogues produced by The Society during our 1990–1991 exhibition season. We feel privileged to receive this trust on behalf of education and scholarship and welcome the presence of The Elizabeth Firestone Graham Foundation here in the Midwest.

It brings significant pleasure to The Society and to its membership to present *The Body*, a montage of the work of writers and artists reflecting important cultural and social concerns. We are grateful to have this forum.

Susanne Ghez
Director

"The Body," March 4–April 21, 1991
The Renaissance Society at The University of Chicago

This catalogue and all 1990–91 publications were made possible with the generous support of The Elizabeth Firestone Graham Foundation.

This project was partially supported by grants from the National Endowment for the Arts, a federal agency; the Illinois Arts Council, a state agency; the CityArts Program of the Chicago Department of Cultural Affairs; and by our Membership. Indirect support has been received from the Institute of Museum Services, a federal agency offering general operating support to the nation's museums. Generous private support has been received from Timothy and Suzette Flood. Major funding for this project has been received from the Lannan Foundation.

ISBN 0–941548–23–6
The Renaissance Society at The University of Chicago
©1991 by The Renaissance Society at The University of Chicago

Designed by Michael Glass Design, Chicago
Edited by Joseph Scanlan
Typeset by Paul Baker Typography, Inc., Evanston, Illinois
Printed by Eastern Press, New Haven, Connecticut
Photos by Tom van Eynde, Forest Park, Illinois